CATS, CRIME & CRÈME BRÛLÉE

A MELTING POT CAFÉ PARANORMAL COZY MYSTERY

NOVELLA

POLLY HOLMES

Western Australia

Copyright

ALSO FROM POLLY HOLMES

Melting Pot Café Series

Pumpkin Pies & Potions #1

Happy Deadly New Year #2

Muffins & Magic #3

Mistletoe, Murder & Mayhem #4

A Deadly Disappearance Down Under # 5

Black Magic Murder #6

Cupcakes & Cauldrons #7

One Hex Too Many #8

Cats, Crime & Crème Brûlée Novella

Cupcake Capers Series

Cupcakes and Conspiracy - Prequel

Cupcakes and Cyanide #1

Cupcakes and Curses #2

Cupcakes and Corpses #3

Murder and Mistletoe #4

Dead Velvet Cupcakes #5

From the Author

Hello my Readers,

Cats, Crime & Crème Brûlée was originally written as part of the All Too Familiar anthology. It is a stand-alone novella linked to The Melting Pot Café series.

Join Evelyn and Tyler as they head to the Noble Crest Assisted Living Facility for their Easter Family Fun Day. The invitation said nothing about jealous lovers, a cover-up, a talking cat statue, and murder!

Elderly resident Madge Bromfield is found dead, and all evidence points to foul play. Besides magic, there's nothing Evelyn loves more than a good mystery, so with her trusty feline familiar in tow, Evelyn puts on her investigator hat, determined to unmask the killer before they strike again.

I hope you enjoy this fun-loving cozy adventure as much as I loved writing it. That's enough from me for now. Turn the page and dive into Evelyn's magical world.

Polly xxoo

CHAPTER ONE

Never in a million years would I have ever imagined my boyfriend with three legs.

I cupped my hands in a circle and brought them up to my mouth and called, "Come on Tyler, you can do it."

I waved at Tyler and Jeffrey as they stood at the starting line of the three-legged race, pumped and ready to run. The huge smile on Jeffrey's face was worth the trip over from Saltwater Cove. An electric buzz shot through my system as I glanced around at all the families that had rocked up for the Noble Crest Assisted Living Easter Family Fun Day.

We'd met Jeffrey a few years back while trying to prove my Aunt Edie's best friend innocent of murder and bonded over chess, of all things. While he wasn't exactly a relative, he'd won our hearts that day, and he's been practically family ever since.

A male nurse with a familiar smile nudged his way up beside me.

"Hi Evelyn."

"Hi Eric."

"It's so good of you and Tyler to come and hang out with Jeffrey and the rest of us today. Great turnout, don't you think?"

A warm glow filled my chest. "Sure is. We wouldn't have missed it for the world."

Between my shifts at The Melting Pot Café and trying to solve a murder or two, or was that three? Who knows, I've lost count. I made sure I blocked the day off work to be here for Jeffrey.

"I hear Tyler has entered the chess competition this year," he said, and giggled.

I nodded.

"Jeffrey has been practicing really hard to beat him. Tyler's going to have his work cut out for him." Eric's attention veered to a kafuffle on the other side of the grassed area where the therapy ponies were situated. "Oh dear, looks like Gladys is causing a bit of a ruckus with the ponies. I swear that woman loves being the centre of attention. Catcha later, Evelyn."

"Bye, Eric. Good luck." I waved as he headed off towards the ponies and then moved up by the starting line.

"Darma…Darma, look at me and my best friend," Jeremy called my way, pointing to Tyler and himself. "We're going to win the race."

I spun to see Jeffrey's older brother, Jeremy, and his wife Darma standing behind me, their arms laden with containers of prepared food. Darma smiled and nodded.

"Way to go, you two. We'll be watching."

"Gee, let me help you with those?" I grabbed two containers from Jeremy's arms before they toppled to the ground. "That was a close call. Better get these to the food table."

"Thanks, Evelyn."

Jeremy smiled, and they followed me to the allocated food table not too far away.

"Sorry, we're late. I miscalculated my cooking times on the strawberry shortcakes."

The mention of the delicious cakes had my mouth watering. "You better make sure I get one of those cakes or there's going to be hell to pay."

Darma giggled and swatted Jeremy across his shoulder. "I told you we should have made extra strawberry shortcakes."

"Did I hear you correctly? You made strawberry shortcakes?" Sasha Blakely stood on the other side of the table, holding three boxes.

Jeremy nodded. "Sure did."

Sasha leaned in and whispered, "I'll trade you some of these Crème Brûlées for your strawberry shortcakes?"

"Goodness, this sounds like a calories fest," I said. Just the thought had my waistline expanding. "Is this your famous Crème Brûlée, Sasha, the ones you bring Arthur every time you visit?"

She nodded. "Dad loves them, but I have to confess I don't make them, my husband Nigel, does. He's a chef. Actually, a Master of Desserts, literally. He even has the Master of Desserts lapel badge to prove it. Won heaps of other awards, too. How else do you think my waistline got this big?"

Awkward.

There was a moment of uncomfortable silence, and then I burst out laughing. "At this rate, I'll be lucky if I don't have to buy a new autumn wardrobe. Sasha, if you're trading some Crème Brûlées for strawberry shortcake, how about I swap you some Crème Brûlées for Aunt Edie's chocolate fudge cake I brought from The Melting Pot, and we'll call it even?"

Sasha's eyes lit up as the sun hits the ocean in the morning. "Deal."

A screeching, booming voice rang out across the grounds, startling most of the attendees, including me.

"Testing...testing. One, two, three. Testing."

I cringed and covered my ears. "Aw, do you think they could turn the volume down?" No sooner had I spoken the words, they did just that.

Great minds think alike, as Aunt Edie would say.

"Sorry about that. I think we have the levels all sorted now." The announcer cleared his throat. "Ladies and gentlemen, boys and girls, welcome to

Noble Crest Assisted Living Easter Family Fun Day." His words were met with a cascade of cheers and wolf-whistles from the crowd. "It's so great to see so many of you here to support the wonderful staff here at Noble Crest and thank them for all the work they do looking after our loved ones."

The announcer continued, revving up the crowd. "I hope you all remembered to bring your Easter Bonnets for the parade later this afternoon and don't forget the Easter Egg Hunt, but right now we're about to start the three-legged race so come on over and join in the fun."

"That's our cue," I said, turning to Darma and Jeremy. My insides were all jittery and I could barely stay in one spot. I made a beeline for the front of the spectator's area calling over my shoulder, "Come on you two, we want a get a good spot near the finish line."

Jeremy's deep voice was not hard to miss. "Right behind you."

I squeezed myself to the front of the crowd close to the finish line and held my hand flat above my eyes to block out the sun while I searched for Tyler and Jeffrey at the other end. My skin tingled under the heat of the morning sun, but also relished in the warmth as it bled into my body.

"There they are." I waved above my head. "Jeffrey...Tyler." The boisterous crowd drowned my voice out, but Tyler knew I'd be watching.

"On your marks," the announcer called. "Get set…go." The starter's pistol pierced the air like a sonic boom kick-starting my heart into overdrive.

The crowd erupted in screams, hollers, and a continuous stream of names yelled. I watched the couples hobble on three legs down the marked lanes towards the finish line. Tyler and Jeffrey were out in front, neck and neck with one other pair. My gut tightened and my hands balled into fists.

"Come on, Tyler. Come on, Jeffrey, this is your win," I yelled continuously, as loud as my vocal cords would allow.

Other cheers and names of competitors disappeared as I centred my focus solely on Tyler and Jeffrey. My heart pounded as they got closer to the end.

"I can't look." I covered my eyes with my hands, leaving a few gaps to peek through. "Oh gosh, this is worse than waiting to try one of Harriet's new food creations." Harriet is one of my best friends, a new witch, and a master chef in the making if she had anything to say about it.

I squinted and looked through the gap in my fingers. They'd pulled out in front. My heart jumped into the back of my throat and my body took over. I jumped up and down, my arms flaying around like octopus legs, screaming their names just as they crossed the finish line to take first place.

I dropped my hands to my knees and sucked in deep breaths before standing upright. "Wow, who knew cheering could be this taxing on the body?"

Darma giggled beside me. "I know, I think I've just about lost my voice from screaming."

The winning couple joined us, and I couldn't wipe the smile off my face. More to the point, I didn't want to.

"Congratulations you two. I knew you could do it."

Still gasping for air, Tyler wiped the beads of sweat from his brow and smiled. "Losing was not an option, but I couldn't have done it without my best mate here." He threw his arm around Jeffrey and they hugged it out.

My throat clogged up as I caught the gleam in Jeffrey's eye.

Jeremy patted Jeffrey's shoulder. "Way to go, bro. I'm so proud of you."

Jeffrey paused and looked blankly at Jeremy, and then it was as though a lightbulb switched on and he knew exactly who he was. He threw his arms around his brother and cried. My throat clogged up with emotion. It still guts me every time I think of Jeffrey's accident when he was a teenager, and how the actions of a drunk driver can have such a devastating effect on one family.

I shook the tingles out of my hands and cleared my throat. "Okay, this requires way too much energy.

Can we move to get ready for the chess competition before I pass out from over-excitement?"

Jeffrey jumped up and down and chanted, "Chess, chess, chess."

Tyler threw me one of his dashing smiles that had my knees weakening and my heart racing. He turned to Jeffrey.

"Hey buddy, shall we go get a few games of practice in before the competition starts?"

He nodded. "I'll race you to the chessboard," Jeffrey said, already on his way up the grassed hill.

"Not if I get there first," Tyler called after him and then took off.

I stood next to Jeremy and Darma and shook my head. "I swear, Tyler would move in here if he could."

All three of us moved off, following the direction the boys took, my shoes cushioned by the soft green grass underfoot. "I can't thank you enough, Evelyn, for all the time you spend with Jeffrey. After Darma's mother passed on, we weren't sure how long it was going to take her to be able to set foot in this place again. This is where we met." He turned and gave his wife a loving hug. "It meant the world to us to know you and Tyler were visiting Jeffrey while we couldn't."

"Yes, thank you," Darma said, behind a haunted smile. "The memories of Mum are so strong here, but then I realised the more I came, the closer I felt to her and it seemed kind of comforting to know that she's still here, in her own way."

"It was our pleasure, honestly. I know we couldn't visit as much as we wanted to, but we tried to get here when we could." We made it up to where they'd set up the chessboards, and I spotted Tyler and Jeffrey in their usual spot over by the entrance under the twinkling party lights of the patio. "I'm going to head over and see if I can get them some refreshments. Do you guys want anything?"

Darma shook her head. "No, thank you."

"I'm good," Jeremy said. "I think I'm going to take Darma to see the therapy ponies before we join you."

I nodded and moved off. Sorrow and hurt ran deep in Darma's eyes, and I knew without a doubt she was still suffering the loss of her mother. My chest ached for her, for I knew exactly what she was going through. Losing my parents at twelve years old was the worst moment of my life, one that will haunt me for the rest of my existence.

A familiar voice muttered behind me. "I tell you, something is not right. Mark my words, they'll never get away with it."

I paused mid-step and caught sight of Madge Bromfield shaking her head. Wrinkles covered her forehead, but I couldn't be certain if it was concern or old age. Either way, for someone who just got engaged, she certainly didn't look happy.

"Hi Madge. Is everything all right?" I asked in my best inquisitive but friendly tone.

She stopped and looked straight through me as though I were glass. Was she even breathing? "Madge, it's Evelyn Grayson. Are you okay?" The longer she stood frozen to the spot, the quicker my pulse picked up.

She blinked a few times and then she tapped her tightened lips with a finger before a smile spread across her face. Gone was the expression of concern replaced with her normal bubbly personality and radiant glow.

"Evelyn, it's so great to see you."

She grabbed my hands and squeezed tight.

"I meant to thank you for the wonderful engagement cake you made for Arthur and me. It truly was the cake of my dreams."

My hands tingled under the pressure of her grip. "It was my pleasure, Madge. You and Arthur make a wonderful couple and to think you met here at Noble Crest. I bet you never imagined falling in love again when you moved in here."

"You got that right. But Arthur, he's—" She paused and her eyes glazed over, her thoughts obviously on her new fiancée. "He's so amazingly generous, so gentle and loving and—"

"Handsome," I said, finishing her sentence.

A giggle escaped her lips and her cheeks glowed with a ruby blush. "He certainly is."

I hope I'm still madly in love at her age.

My thoughts drifted back to her earlier mutterings. "Madge, I was wondering what you meant when you said something wasn't right, and they'll never get away with it. Who won't get away with what?"

Madge paled and stood stock still, then broke into a semi-controlled laugh. "Pfft, oh don't mind me. Everything's fine, love. It was just silly old me thinking way too hard in my old age. Now I've something to take care of and you have a chess competition to watch."

She threw her arms around my shoulders and squeezed.

"Thank you again for the engagement cake. See you later." And she was off, bouncing towards the main building.

I rubbed my forehead and forcibly flattened the growing wrinkles. "Did I miss something? Guess not." I shrugged my shoulders and high-tailed it to watch the impending chess challenge.

A sizeable crowd had gathered around the chess tables, all waiting eagerly to see who would make it through to the final few rounds. An emptiness filled the base of my gut and I rubbed the back of my neck. Eric was right, Jeffrey had been practicing. It was a kick in the guts when we found out he suffered brain damage in the car accident. Life can be cruel sometimes.

"Come on, Tyler. You've got this," I muttered under my breath as I watched a myriad of expressions pass over his face. He frowned, he smiled, he twitched, he frowned again. It's not like him to doubt his chess-playing abilities.

Resting my elbow on a nearby plant box, I leaned in closer to get a better look at the board. If it were me, I'd move my knight and swipe Jeffrey's castle. I bit my bottom lip, hard, and held my breath as Tyler reached for his knight. His move cut short by an ear-piercing scream that sent my blood curdling.

CHAPTER TWO

"What was that?" My gaze caught Tyler's, and it was as though he read my mind.

"That can't be good," he said. "Sounds like a scream we've heard one too many times before."

There were mutters and gasps from the spectators, each frantically looking around, searching for the source of the disturbance.

"That sounded like a scream from a horror movie."

"…oh no, what happened?"

"…I can't imagine what would make someone scream like that…"

I can…a dead body.

The image had my stomach knotting so fast bile rose to the back of my throat. The gentleman running the chess competition stepped up and held his arms out.

"Okay everyone, let's all calm down. I'm sure the staff has it all under control. It's probably just an innocent accident. I say we not let it spoil our wonderful day here at Noble Crest and continue with our competition. I'm sure they will let us know in due course if there is a problem."

Tyler's eyes widened and his head tilted towards the open doors that led to the main building. He mouthed the word, "Go."

He didn't have to tell me twice. My interest was already piqued. I nodded and headed off towards the entrance, only to run into the back of a noisy crowd trying to push and shove their way inside past the nurses working to keep everyone calm.

"This is getting me nowhere." I backed up, excusing myself and moved to the other side of the grassed area where the crowd seemed oblivious to the commotion at the main entrance. I held my breath and casually walked over to the fountain beside the alternate entry door and pretended to admire the honeysuckle flowers adorning the wall.

Big mistake. The sweet succulent scent stuck in the back of my nostrils and initiated a row of hay fever induced sneezes. After the ninth consecutive sneeze, my head pounded like a jackhammer and my blocked nose made breathing almost impossible. I rubbed my forehead. "Seriously? That's all I need, a bout of hay fever to wreak havoc on my day."

Not if I can help it.

I tried to sniff and my chest tightened as I moved behind a trellis of exquisite dainty pink and white roses out of sight of the crowd. Magic was not a secret in Saltwater Cove, but here in Hallows Creek, I wasn't so sure, especially with so many visiting families from towns unknown. Checking the coast was clear of party goers, I put my right hand to my temple and held the other a few inches from my left temple and said, "Pain and suffering come to rest, leave my body at my request. With this spell please disappear, pain be gone, and all is clear."

My fingertips tingled and a thawing sensation worked its way down my fingers to my palms. A bluish-green twisting beam of light circled my head and a transient flash of white scattered dots passed before my eyes and then they were gone, along with my blocked nose and hay fever. I breathed in a huge lungful of air through my nostrils and basked in the ability to breathe clearly. "Ah, that's more like it."

Steering clear of the honeysuckle bush, I headed towards the door on the other side of the fountain. Turning the cool metal doorhandle, I eased my shoulder up against the solid wood door and pushed, but it failed to budge. I tried my access card on the panel, but still no luck.

"Darn, they must have these doors on a different access code."

"I may be a graduate witch, but there is one spell I've mastered." I glued my eyes to the lock, and I kept my hand securely on the door handle and the other a few inches away. The tips of my fingers tingled like a rush of pins and needles. "What once was under lock and key, with this spell I now set free. Once done with it, then let it be, return it under lock and key." A rainbow of glittery sparkles danced around my fingers and over the lock, and a sharp click pierced the air as it disengaged.

"Bingo." I bit down hard on the inside of my cheek as I turned the door handle and pushed it open. A buzz of electricity ignited through me. I silently stepped in, eyeing the empty corridor. As soon as the door closed behind me, a sharp click initiated the locking mechanism into place. A smile spread across my face.

It's times like these I love being a witch.

The corridor's overwhelming, sterile scent embedded itself in the back of my throat. Swallowing hard, I held my breath and moved with conviction toward the location the scream came from, the same direction as Jeffrey's room. I spied a vase of flowers sitting on a lone cart outside the utility room. A perfect distraction if I ever saw one.

I picked up the vase and made sure there was no card, then restarted my journey towards Jeffrey's room. I turned the corner and jerked backwards and a gasp left me as I ran into Isla, the Noble Crest receptionist. Literally.

"Isla, oh my goodness, I am so sorry. I didn't see you there," I said, in my best concerned voice. "That was a close call. I'm glad you didn't wear these flowers all over you." As I brushed off the stray petals and baby's breath that landed on my shirt, I caught sight of her red, swollen eyes. I opened my mouth to ask what was wrong, but I needn't worry. It blurted from her lips in one stream of verbal diarrhoea.

"Oh gosh, Evelyn, it was awful, just awful." Sniff, sniff, and she wiped her nose with the back of her sleeve.

Eww, I think that's why they invented disposable tissues.

"I've never been so horrified in all my life. I mean, I know I work in an assisted living home and there are old people here as well as young, and I expected to eventually come face to face with death. Death by old age not..." She paused and shook her head. "But this was different. She just lay there...staring at me."

"Who?" My pulse jacked up as I waited for the crucial bit of missing information.

Isla swallowed and fresh tears brimmed the edge of her eyes. "She was all twisted and the blood, oh the blood."

"Who was it, Isla?" I asked, my pulse now running its own marathon.

She squeezed her eyes shut as though she were trying to block it out of her mind. "That poor woman, and just after making one of the most important decisions of her life."

I pressed my lips together and grabbed Isla's shoulders, holding her still. I looked her directly in the eyes and asked once more, "Who, Isla, who was it? I know it was a shock, but who are you talking about?"

She paled. "Madge Bromfield."

Madge Bromfield? No, that can't be right. I saw her not long ago.

My chest seized as though it were stuck with a lightning bolt. "Are you sure it was Madge's body you saw? Maybe you were mistaken."

She brushed my hands from her shoulders and stepped back, crossing her arms. The warm spring air turned in an instant and I shivered as an icy chill crossed between us. Her eyes squinted and if she were a witch, she probably would have vaporised me where I stood.

"I know you think I'm some dumb receptionist who only answers phones and takes appointments, but I am way smarter than that, Evelyn. I'm not stupid. I know what I saw, and I saw Madge Bromfield laying on the floor of her bathroom with a bloodied gash in the side of her head."

My jaw dropped, and my throat tightened to the point of pain. I swallowed and shook my head at her outburst.

"Isla, I have no idea what you're talking about. I never said or implied that you're dumb or stupid. Never. I don't know why you would ever think that. I happen to think you're pretty smart, but if I have done something to make you think ill of me, please tell me so I can correct it immediately."

Her arms slowly dropped, and her eyebrows squished together. "So, you didn't say that I was a snarking know it all that had less brains than a goldfish?"

"Good heavens, no," I said, her words as good as stabbed me in the heart. "How…why…where did you come up with such a crazy notion?"

"The last time I was in Saltwater Cove, I'd called into Salty Snips to pick up some more hair shampoo for my mum and I overheard a few customers talking. They mentioned you and me and although I couldn't hear everything, it was clear what they said. I assumed they were talking about me and since yours was the only name I heard, I thought you said it."

Heat invaded my neck and cheeks, and I sucked in a deep breath, steadying my racing pulse. "Isla, I don't know what was being said and why either of our names was mentioned, but you can't always believe everything you hear. There is an abundance of gossips in Saltwater Cove who love nothing more than to talk about others, especially at Salty Snips. That's prime real estate for gossips. I promise you, I never said that or anything like it. You are a smart, beautiful young woman with the world at her feet."

A smile warmed her expression.

"Just promise me, if you hear anything like that again, come and ask me before assuming it was me who said it."

"Okay, sorry. I guess I should have known Tyler would never go out with someone so shallow."

I should hope not.

My back stiffened, and a strange sensation washed over me. It had a familiarity to it I couldn't put my finger on. I shook it off. "How about we get back to the part where you saw Madge on the floor?"

She nodded. "Like everyone else, I heard the scream and raced to see what was wrong. I found one of the nurses hyperventilating and crying. Her hands were shaking, and she was muttering and mumbling something I couldn't understand."

"Then what happened?"

"The owner and manager arrived and shooed us out." Isla fiddled with the collar of her uniform shirt, twisting it between her fingers. "The nurse went into the staff lounge and I came down here. I was heading out for some fresh air away from the crowd that had gathered at the main entry door when I ran into you. That's the first dead body I've seen. The blood, Evelyn. Why was there so much blood?"

She paled, and the glassiness in her eyes was like a warning before the storm hit. It's a classic I'm-going-to-be-sick-all-over-your-shoes expression. I caught sight of a sink and a chair in the utility room. Ushering Isla inside to the chair, I saw she moved without too much effort and after I brought her a glass of water, her expression normalised.

"Feeling better?"

She nodded. "Thanks. Sorry."

"Pfft," I said, brushing my arm as though I were swatting a fly from my shoulder. "Don't be sorry. Not everyone can stomach seeing a dead body."

"You can." She looked me in the eye. "Tyler was telling me how Prudence McAvoy's body was found in your pond on New Year's Eve and how you had to use your witch powers to find the real killer."

An icy chill danced up my spine at the memory of my high school arch nemesis' body laying half submerged in the outdoor pond at The Melting Pot. Not the best night of my life. I shook the unwarranted chill from my bones and concentrated on our current dead body.

I crouched down to eye level with Isla and gifted her my best I'm-here-for-you-smile. "Let's forget about New Year's Eve and focus on the here and now, on Madge. Madge didn't deserve what happened to her. I'd hate to have Madge be on the end of a supernatural occurrence. If somehow her death was associated with witchcraft, I'd never forgive myself if I didn't investigate and learn the truth. And I'm positive the rest of the world doesn't really need to know about it. Will you help me, Isla? Will you help me get to the bottom of Madge Bromfield's murder?"

A spark ignited in her eyes, and she shot off the chair. "Hell yes."

That's the girl. "Okay. First things first. I need to see the body. Can you get me close enough to have a look at it?" I stood up and a rush of light-headedness hit me. The familiarity of it went as quick as it came.

What was that?

Isla's hand flew to her mouth and she bit excessively on her fingernail. "Um, that could be a problem. She was found on the floor in her bathroom. I mean, they probably have it all cordoned off by now."

"Think, Isla," I said, a little sharper than I expected. "There must be another way around to her room. I'm sure you know this place like the back of your hand."

Her eyes widened, and she snapped her fingers. "Yes, you're right. There is another way round and I can take you there."

"Great, let's go." No sooner had we stepped outside the utility room than a feline of the familiar kind stopped us in our path.

Miss Saffron, what are you doing here?

CHAPTER THREE

"This day just keeps getting better by the second," I said, folding my arms and tilting my head to look at my trusty familiar. "Miss Saffron, what on earth brought you to Noble Crest today of all days?"

"Miss Saffron?" Isla asked, looking from the cat to me and then back again.

"Oh, excuse me. Miss Saffron, this is Isla." I paused, looking at Isla's dazed expression. "Isla, this is Miss Saffron."

Miss Saffron's golden eyes glowed. She fluttered her eyelashes at the redhead and took what looked like an elegant bow. Isla stared down at the cat and let out a giggle.

"If I didn't know better, I'd say that cat understood exactly what you said, and then bowed."

"Very observant, isn't she?" echoed Miss Saffron snidely as she wiped her whiskers with her paw.

"As a matter of fact, she is."

Isla turned and looked at me.

"Who is what?"

I slapped my forehead. "Oh sorry. I forgot you don't know."

"Don't know what?" she asked, her expression a picture of pure innocence.

"You know I'm a witch, right?"

Isla nodded.

"It's not uncommon for a witch to have a familiar," I said, working out the best way to explain it without being too complicated.

Her brow creased. "A familiar?"

"A familiar, my dear." Miss Saffron paused, sitting back on her haunches. "Is a gorgeous being full of wisdom and knowledge here to guide the witch in her magical workings."

Knowing full well I was the only one who could hear Miss Saffron, I repeated what she said without the sarcasm.

"Basically, they're an animal here to help witches, kind of like a spirit guide. They have the knowledge and wisdom to help a witch tackle the supernatural world and it just so happens Miss Saffron and I can communicate telepathically. She can also speak out loud, but I'm the only one that can hear her. As can any of my blood relatives."

"That is the coolest thing I've ever heard." Isla's eyes lit up like sparklers. "And here I was thinking they were imaginary and only *Sabrina the Teenage Witch* had one, albeit an annoying one at that."

"Wash your mouth out, young lady," Miss Saffron snapped.

That's enough. I don't know why you're here, but now is not the time. There has been a murder, and Isla has agreed to help me find out if it has a supernatural connection.

Miss Saffron turned her golden eyes my way and gave me a wink.

"That's exactly why I'm here. My familiar radar was spiked, and my curiosity got the better of me. Something's not right here. I can feel it in my cat bones."

Oh, okay, well, stay close by and give me a heads-up if you find anything untoward.

Turning back to Isla, I clasped my hands together at my waist and smiled. "Let's get back to what we were doing. You were going to take me another way round to Madge's room, remember?"

"That's right. This way," she said, pointing down a darkened corridor. She'd only taken a few steps ahead of me when she spun around. "Will Miss Saffron be joining us?"

I nodded. "Will that be a problem?"

"Not at all, but if asked, it would be wise to say she's a therapy cat brought in for today's event. That way it will avoid all unnecessary questions."

"Therapy cat? Well, I never…a therapy cat of all things. I will not become someone's glorified play toy."

Shh, play along. I'll take it if it gets you past the authorities.

"No problem. Thanks, Isla, for the quick thinking."

* * *

By the time we'd made it around the back way to Madge's room the crowd had thinned, and the area cordoned off. A soft white haze lit the carpet outside the room, clearly showing her room door still open. Fingers crossed; it stayed that way.

There were only a few staff members left, including a doctor, one fancy dressed woman and a man in a suit. They were all standing a few metres this side of Madge's room in a semi-huddle, deep in conversation, all facing the other direction, which worked great for us.

"Who are they?"

Isla held up her hand and whispered behind it. "That's the owners of Noble Crest, Adele and Joseph Ramsey. I guess someone called in the big guns. What do you suppose they're talking about?"

I gave her a sideways glance that clearly read; Are-you-kidding-me? "My guess is the dead body."

"Right, of course."

She turned away, but not before I caught sight of the crimson blush invading her cheeks.

Miss Saffron stepped forward and arched her back, her ears pointing straight up like a stiff piece of cardboard. A deep guttural purr bellowed from her before she turned and gazed my way. "I have an idea. We'll never get in there to have a look if you two go barging down like a marching band demanding answers."

Since when have you ever known me to be in a marching band?

Miss Saffron rolled her eyes. "You know what I mean. May I suggest a little more tact? I'll head down and take a look around, out of sight, of course, and since you're set on the therapy cat idea, you and Isla can follow a few minutes later pretending to look for me."

And that's why you're my familiar. Cute, sassy, and smart.

I turned to Isla and placed a comforting hand on her forearm. "It's okay. We have a plan. Miss Saffron will head down first and take a look inside Madge's room, unnoticed, of course. You and I will follow a few minutes later. If they question our sudden appearance, you can say since you found the body, you thought they might want to chat to you. I'll say I'm looking for Miss Saffron and happened to run into you on the way."

"I like it." She nodded and glanced back towards Madge's room. "Poor Madge. I hope the person who did that to her is strung up by their ankles and shot."

"I couldn't agree more," I said, nodding at Miss Saffron. "But I'll happily settle for jail."

Miss Saffron licked her paw before nodding, then moved off down the corridor. She took each step cautiously, sticking close to the wall, her tail whipping from side to side. With everyone's attention firmly caught in the private discussion, she slinked past them into Madge's room without any issue.

Atta girl.

I kept my eye on the group, and as time ticked over, it was clear they were getting restless. "Are you ready?" I asked Isla.

She nodded and rolled her shoulders back. "As ready as I'll ever be. Let's do this."

"Follow my lead," I said. Isla nodded and fell into step beside me. My chest tightened and my body tensed with each step closer to the closed group. There was a lot that sounded like gibberish, but two words stood out above the rest. The 'M' word followed by the word 'cover-up'.

Not on my watch.

I stopped and faced Isla, pulling her off to the side behind a metal storage unit, my pulse racing.

Her eyes widened, and her jaw dropped. "What's wrong?" she mouthed.

My stomach churned at the mere thought of a cover-up. "Change of plans. We're going in with a splash. You in? For Madge."

Her back stiffened, as did her upper lip. "I'm in. For Madge. What do you want me to do?"

"Head down and get them talking, but keep them from looking this way. Ask if they want your side of the story. Remind them you were one of the few people to see the body. Just try to keep them talking to see if they'll spill any more information. And don't let them shut the door to her room."

"That I can do."

Isla smiled and brushed pretend wrinkles from her uniform shirt and moved off. As she approached the group, her hands moved between twisting her fingers together at her sides and touching her face. She sure looked anxious, but the subtle change in her voice confirmed my suspicion. Holding my breath, I edged close enough to hear the conversation without being noticed.

"Oh my gosh, Mr and Mrs Ramsey, I'm so glad you're here." Isla carefully placed herself on the other side of the group but kept her pacing and shuffling consistent.

"Isla, what are you doing here?" Adele Ramsey demanded. Standing tall in her fancy business suit, she looked Isla up and down and tutted. "This is a closed area. I'm not sure why you have left your position at reception."

"I'm sorry, Mrs Ramsey. I just can't believe what happened to poor old Madge Bromfield. It's just terrible and when I saw her bloodied body lying on the floor, her cold eyes were staring at me. It was horrible."

I watched as Isla's torso shivered and she wiped her eyes with the back of her hand as though she were crying. Maybe she was.

Joseph Ramsey cleared his throat and threw his wife a hard smile. "It's all right, Adele."

He turned to Isla, placed a hand on her shoulder and squeezed. An eerie shiver crept across my shoulder blades.

Creep. Note to self: in future, keep an eye on Joseph Ramsey when he's around Isla.

He continued, "I can't imagine what you're going through. The shock of seeing poor Madge that way. It must have been awful."

Isla's lips trembled, and she nodded. "It was. I knew you'd have some questions and I want to help find the person who did that to Madge."

"What makes you think it wasn't an accident?" the doctor asked.

Isla took a step back and her head drew back quickly. "That could be no accident. You saw her. How could Madge have done that to herself? There was so much blood on the back of her head and all over the bathroom floor."

"Yes, there was, but Dr Castillo's preliminary thoughts lean towards accident," Adele said, looking pleased as punch with her summation.

Accident? You can't be serious?

"Evelyn." Miss Saffron's voice startled my thoughts. "You better get in here. If what I'm looking at is correct, this was no accident. It was murder."

Murder, are you sure?

"As sure as I'm standing here, one hundred and nine years old."

Hang on, I'm on my way.

I expelled all my breath, forcing it out as Miss Saffron's words hardened my stomach. Time to rehash my acting skills. Stepping out into the corridor, I headed toward the gathered group. I took in Isla's emotional state and my muscles clenched as I appeared, placing my arm around her shoulders. I gave her my best sympathetic frown.

"Oh, you poor thing. Are you all right?"

"Where did you come from?" Adele asked, glaring like Grumpy dwarf.

She paused and her intense gaze searched the corridor from whence I came and then back to me.

"She's fine, just had a little fright, that's all. Can I help you with something?" Adele moved to step towards Madge's room and my breathing accelerated.

"Oh my," I said, shooting out my hand and grabbing her arm, freezing her to the spot. "I sure hope so. I'm looking for my cat."

Adele's gaze drilled into me before dropping to my hand and clenching her forearms.

"Your cat?"

I pursed my lips and nodded, holding my hand firmly in place. "She's a therapy cat. She got spooked when the terrible scream happened not long ago and now I can't find her. Have you seen her around? She's a silver tipped Chausie with the most gorgeous golden almond-shaped eyes. They say the Chausie breed is a distant cousin of the miniature cougar."

"Can you hear that?" Isla asked, biting her bottom lip with her eyes wide. "It's a cat and I think it's coming from Madge's room."

There was a moment of stillness where everyone stood frozen to the spot, the tense air thick as molasses. Then, as if on cue, we all moved to the entry door double time. I beat the rest for a prime position in the entryway. The sight of poor Madge laying mangled on the floor of her bathroom in a pool of blood caught my breath. The two rather large gashes on her head did not go unnoticed. I guess you never get used to the cold, frozen image of a dead body. At least I won't.

"Did you see her injuries?" Miss Saffron asked.

I sure did. There's no way they are self-inflicted.

"Agreed, but there's more to this scene than meets the eye. I just can't put my paw on it."

"Oh, poor Madge," Isla said, her hand flying to her gapping mouth and glistening tears threatening to trickle down her cheeks.

"Poor Madge is right." My breathing sped, and I turned to the doctor. "I know it has not long happened, but I cannot believe you have left her on the floor for all to see. You could have at least covered her with a sheet."

He paled and blinked several times before darting across the room and ripping the top sheet off her bed and covering her body.

Adele edged her way in and planted herself between me and the body. Folding her arms across her chest, she pursed her lips and huffed.

"Thank you for your concern. Now if you wouldn't mind leaving, there is a lot to do."

A soft meow echoed from the other side of the room and all eyes turned to where Miss Saffron was sitting on her haunches.

"Miss Saffron, there you are," I said, side-stepping Adele and shooting to the other side of the room. I bent down and picked up my furball and snuggled her to my chest. "How many times have I told you to stay close to me at all times, you cheeky little cat?"

Miss Saffron purred and rubbed the top of her head back and forth under my chin, playing along with the charade. I mustered up my best innocent smile and flashed my lashes at Adele.

"I swear, sometimes this cat thinks she's the boss."

Isla cleared her throat. "Gee, that was lucky you found her. We probably should leave you to it. We don't want to be in the way when the police get here."

Adele stepped aside and threw me an evil glare to rival Cinderella's stepmother. She held her hand out towards the open door.

"The police won't be necessary; we'll be handling this situation in-house."

"In-house? What do you mean 'in-house?'" I asked, the heat rising up my neck.

"Not that it's any of our concern." Joseph Ramsey's shoulders stiffened. "But accidents like this happen all the time around old people. They're frail, brittle, and sometimes their injuries are self-inflicted through no fault of their own."

A low hissing growl murmured against my neck. "Madge's injuries were hardly self-inflicted."

I couldn't agree more.

Isla stepped forward, her arms folded across her chest and her fingers tapped a regular beat against her elbow. "Isn't it our policy that all deaths, suspicious or not, are reported to the police? At least that's what my training taught me, and I don't think it's changed."

I bumped shoulders with Isla, providing a united front. "I know for a fact, Detective Huxton of the Saltwater Cove police department is close by and would be happy to call in. I have his number. I'd be happy to call him if you don't."

My gut tightened as the air thickened. Adele and Joseph exchanged a guarded look between them, but it was the doctor who broke the edgy silence. "Very well." He turned towards his employers. "It's probably best that this situation is handled by a professional anyway and Detective Huxton is highly regarded in his field."

Thank goodness.

"It's settled then," I said, pulling out my phone from my back pocket. I punched in Detective Huxton's number and held it out towards Adele and

Joseph. "Here, I've already dialled the number for you. I'm sure he'd be happy to make an unscheduled stop on the way back to Saltwater Cove."

CHAPTER FOUR

"Tell me again, Evelyn, why do I find you mixed up in another dead body scenario?" Detective Huxton asked, his head shaking with each word spoken.

"Hey, that's not fair." I pressed my lips together and sucked in a few steadying breaths through my nose. "I am not always mixed up with dead bodies."

His eyebrows shot up, and his eyes narrowed. "Really?"

I bit my bottom lip, and my thoughts drifted. There was that time Harriet found Camille Stenson's dead body, and I found my arch nemesis dead in The Melting Pot Café pond on New Year's Eve. I suppose you could count Seraphina Morgan from the Coven of the Night Moon's lifeless body. I shrugged.

"Okay, maybe I have been around my fair share of dead bodies, but it's not like I planned it or anything. Besides, this one is different."

"How so?" he asked, rubbing his chin.

"Adele and Joseph Ramsey weren't going to call the police. If it wasn't for me insisting they call you, Madge's death would have been deemed an accident and brushed under the carpet, and everyone would be none the wiser. Now to me, that says they have something to hide." I glanced down at the furball snuggled between my feet, listening intently to the conversation. "Miss Saffron and I are sure her death was anything but accidental."

"I see." He paced the corridor, chancing a look now and then down at the police tape blocking Madge's room. "Why are you here?"

I rolled my eyes and shook my head. "To make sure the person who did this to Madge gets what's coming to them."

"No." He paused and scratched his cheek. "I mean, why are you here at Noble Crest's Easter Family Fun Day? It's not like you have family here."

"It's Jeffrey." Warm fuzzies filled my chest. "Jeffrey Allen. Tyler and I met him when we were trying to find Camille Stenson's killer and he kind of grew on us. We've been visiting him off and on ever since. We promised we'd be here today and for Madge's sake, I'm glad we were."

He flipped open his notebook and tapped the end of his pen on the blank page. "Did you know Madge well?"

"As well as any other patient in Jeffrey's wing. She and Arthur had just got engaged, and as far as I knew, they were happy. This is going to destroy him. Everyone loved Madge."

Without lifting his eyes from the page, he muttered, "Not everyone."

"What did you find when you examined the body?" I asked, my curiosity getting the better of me. "Apart from the two bloodied gashes on the back of her head that I bet killed her."

"It's an open investigation, Evelyn. As yet, I'm not sure what is going on here. I'll have a better idea once I hear back from the coroner and start asking questions."

"Do you think you'll have time to do this case justice with Constable Antonio out of town on a course and your own cases back at Saltwater Cove?"

He paused and tapped his notebook in his palm and gave a strong, decisive nod. "You can count on it. Every case I take on gets my full attention, but I wouldn't say no to any help or information you can provide me. We seem to work best when we keep the two-way street open."

I gifted him a smile and saw respect in his unwavering eye contact. "Two-way street it is. I don't have much yet, but I did see Madge earlier today."

"And?" His notepad froze in the palm of his hand.

A wave of nausea washed over me, remembering our earlier conversation.

"She was walking past me, and I happened to hear her say, 'I tell you; something is not right. Mark my words, they'll never get away with it.' I have no idea who will get away with what, but if I were to guess, I'd say they silenced her in the most awful way possible."

He nodded. "I have to agree with you on that point."

I rubbed my forehead as my thoughts of earlier in the day flashed through my mind. "And to add to the day's mystery, Miss Saffron turned up out of the blue. Apparently, her 'familiar radar was spiked', whatever that means. She said something wasn't right. She could feel it in her cat bones."

"Thank you, Evelyn. It's a start." He tucked his notebook back into his jacket pocket. "I'll take it from here. My suggestion is you look into what caught Miss Saffron's attention and get back to me if it pertains to Madge's death."

"Deal." The nausea swirling around in my stomach dropped like a lead weight as I spun on my heel, heading back to inform Tyler of my unwelcomed discovery.

* * *

Jeffrey's attention was on Jeremy and Darma and they appeared deep in conversation, hands flaying around like animated cartoon characters. By the time I'd updated Tyler on the tragic end to Madge's life, a tinge of green edged his cheeks. He visibly gulped down the lump in his throat.

"Poor old, Madge. I can't imagine who would have done such a horrible thing to such a beautiful old lady."

My hand found his, and I intertwined our fingers together, sending him a jolt of warmth and support. "I know it's a shock, but there's more. Something strange is going on here and with the sudden appearance of Miss Saffron, I am sure there are magical elements at play."

His hands stiffened in mine and he pulled back, his eyes narrowing. "What are you thinking?"

Wrestling with the piercing pain stabbing the back of my neck, I sucked in a deep breath and brushed my hair off my face.

"I'm thinking that I'm not leaving here until I have some answers. If there is magic at play, especially dark magic, then we need to get to the bottom of it before anyone else loses their life."

"Agreed," he said, bolting from his chair. "Count me in. What's our next step?"

I joined him standing looking around at the crowds, who appeared to have returned to the normal activities. I bet they don't even know what's happened. The nausea in my stomach was now replaced with an abundance of growing knots. I tensed and pushed up on my tippy toes to reach Tyler's ear.

"We look for a murderer and the best place to start is at the scene of the crime."

Tyler stepped aside and held one arm open and winked. "Lead the way."

He sounded so forceful and sexy when he took charge. A bubbly giggle worked its way up from my belly. My lips pressed together.

"Sorry, this is no time to be laughing."

My eyelids lowered as his lips descended on mine in a delicate kiss and my insides turned to jelly. He deepened the kiss and the taste of his lips sent warm shivers through me. Breathless, I broke the kiss, and he rested his forehead against mine.

"Thank you."

"For what?" he whispered, threading his arms around my waist.

"For taking my mind off the awful situation with Madge and allowing me to remember that there is beauty in the world."

"Gee, I had no idea I was that good."

Tyler smirked, and the glint in his gorgeous blue eyes went straight to my heart.

"I miss kissing you, that's all."

He battered his eyelashes at me, and I play punched him in the stomach. He squirmed and gasped. "You're incorrigible. Let's go." I grabbed his hand and headed towards the main house.

We'd only made it half-way to Madge's room when Detective Huxton, sporting a beaming smile stopped us.

"Evelyn, I was on my way to find you. Good to see you again, Tyler." They shook hands, and then he turned his attention to me.

"Oh."

"I'm happy to say we have a person of interest we're holding for questioning," he said, pleased as punch with himself.

My head spun with giddiness at the ease with which the words left his lips. "Already? That was quick. Who?"

"Katrina Perez, one of the nurses here at Noble Crest." He nodded towards the room at the end of the corridor. "She was edgy when questioned and her story kept changing. She admits she has no alibi and maintains she was alone in the medical room dispensing medications at the time. And…" He paused and checked his notes. "According to Adele Ramsey, she has been suspected of stealing prescription drugs and her harsh interactions with patients, including Madge, have been reported on several occasions. She's had several verbal warnings and was on her first written warning. She gave permission for her locker to be searched where we found some of the said stolen drugs."

"What?" My eye caught a slight movement down the corridor behind him and my pulse raced at the sight of Miss Saffron edging her way towards Madge's room.

Miss Saffron, for goodness' sake, don't get caught.

"Like I'm going to let that happen. Trust me," her voice whispered in my head.

"That sounds pretty convenient to me," Tyler said, disgruntled.

Detective Huxton's eyes narrowed, and he took a step closer. "Maybe so, but it's not all hearsay alone. I may be a detective, but I'm a Leodian first, which affords me the ability to hold an object and see its past."

"And did you?" I asked, the heat in my neck rising.

"That I did. On searching her locker, I found her ID badge and was able to get a reading from it, and not a nice one. I'm afraid."

My stomach heaved, and I squeezed Tyler's hand. "I'm not sure I'm following."

"The vision was pretty clear," he said, one eyebrow raised. "Madge and Katrina in a heated argument, both ladies giving as good as they could get. Leads me to believe there was bad blood between them. For all I know, this could be a revenge killing."

A revenge killing? As if.

My chest burned, and I opened my mouth to rebut his comment, but he'd moved off towards the double doors at the opposite end of the corridor, calling over his shoulder. "I'm not going to get anything done chatting here. Time is ticking away. If you need me, I'll be taking a few more statements and then I'll be heading to the station."

The image of his back retreating towards the doors grated on my nerves. I folded my arms across my chest and kept my gaze glued to his back until he was out of sight.

"A revenge killing is the most preposterous thing I've ever heard…and from Katrina? I know the woman is a bit headstrong, but I can't believe she would resort to murder over a heated argument."

"I agree with you, but the evidence always speaks louder than a witch's hunch," Tyler said with a casual shrug.

"Evidence?" I glared at Tyler. I clicked my fingers and pointed at him. "That's it. The only way we're going to find Madge's killer is to find the right evidence, and that means combing her room with a fine-tooth comb, so to speak."

He nodded. "Agreed."

Adrenaline pumped through my body as I approached Miss Saffron sitting under the police tape blocking Madge's room from the public. Tyler stood close by, his warm breath skimming the delicate skin on the back of my neck, and I took a moment to soak up his warmth. I eyed the door handle, my heartbeat throbbing inside my chest. The sudden stillness of the corridor battered against a thunderous storm raging inside my head.

"Are we going to do this?" Tyler asked. "Or have you changed your mind?"

"Hardly," I said. Turning the metal doorknob in my warm hand, I ducked under the police tape and stood frozen in the centre of the room. An eerie chill goose bumped my skin, causing the minute hairs on the back of my neck to stand at attention.

A shiver ran down my spine. "Why do I feel like someone is watching us?" I muttered under my breath, looking down at Miss Saffron.

"I have the same feeling," Miss Saffron said, slinking across the room towards Madge's bed. "If someone is here, and they're of the magical realm, you and I will be the only ones who can sense them."

I shook the tension from my hands and planted them on my hips. "Right, let's get started. Keep your eyes peeled for anything out of place."

Madge was so meticulous about cleanliness. Everything in its place and a place for everything. Except the blood smeared down the door and on the bathroom floor where her body once lay. Nausea bubbled in my belly and I pinched my lips together.

"I'm not sure this is getting us any closer to finding Madge's killer," Tyler said, running a hand through his tousled hair.

I jumped at the guarded purr of Miss Saffron. "Who said that?" she hissed.

"Who said what?" I asked, looking from Tyler to Miss Saffron. Her ears spiked straight up, and her protective hiss echoed around the room.

"Evelyn, be careful. We're not alone." She hissed.

"What do you mean, we're not alone?" I pried, my gaze darting from one place to another, searching for an intruder.

"What is going on, Evelyn?" Tyler asked, a frown creasing his brow. "I really hate it that you are the only one who can hear Miss Saffron speak. I know it's a witch thing, but it makes following your conversation pretty hard."

"Okay, this charade has gone on long enough. Show yourself, whatever you are."

Miss Saffron sprang from the bed and dropped to the ground in a sneaky low to the ground crawl. She placed herself between me and Madge's dresser. Her tail twitched and her gaze rooted to the items delicately arranged on top.

"Evelyn, any chance you can fill me in?" Tyler asked, pointing at Miss Saffron's defensive position. "Your familiar is acting very strangely...even for a cat."

You would too if there was another animal hiding in plain sight.

What the? Are you sure?

The air squeezed from my chest

As sure as I'm talking to you telepathically right now.

My protective instincts kicked in and I stepped in front of Tyler, searching the room for any sort of animal, but if they were here, I couldn't see them.

"Are you sure your familiar radar is not playing tricks on you?"

Miss Saffron bounded up onto the bedside table and then on to the top of the dresser, baring her teeth in a snarl towards the black porcelain sleeping cat statue in the centre. Her back arched and her hind legs stretched, and she circled the statue like a cougar taunting her prey.

"What's got into you?" I asked, taking a step toward the dresser.

"Gotcha," she hissed, stopping by the side of the statue. "Explain yourself." The air thickened as an awkward silence filled the room. I stood, shaking my head at Miss Saffron's antics. There usually was a reason behind her bizarre behaviour, although she was taking her time with an explanation.

I huffed, fed up with not knowing what was going on. "Who are you talking to?"

"The statue," she said.

"The statue?" I repeated, tilting my head and staring her down. "The statue of a sleeping cat? Are you serious?"

Miss Saffron's golden oval eyes glowed, and she stood guarding the cat statue as though her life depended on it.

"Evelyn, I'd like you to meet Shadow. Apparently, Madge picked him up in a yard sale many years ago."

"I'm confused," Tyler said, rubbing his forehead, his gaze stuck on my furry familiar. "Is Miss Saffron talking to that cat statue?"

"Of course not." I swatted Tyler on the shoulder and a muffled laugh escaped my lips. His question sounded more ludicrous by the second. Didn't it? A sudden wave of heat washed over me, and my hand flew to my cheek. Heat pummelled my hand as Tyler's question replayed in my mind.

Please tell me you're not going crazy in your old age and you think you can talk to porcelain statues?

"No, I'm not going crazy, but yes, I can talk to this porcelain statue and that's because it's not a real cat statue. It's a familiar who was caught in the middle of a witch spell war and was turned into a sleeping cat statue by mistake, and thanks to Madge, has been sitting on this dresser for the better part of nine years."

CHAPTER FIVE

My jaw dropped. They were not the words I expected to escape Miss Saffron's lips. "Well, that was totally unexpected."

"What was unexpected?" Tyler asked, his frustration clearly radiating through his tone.

I turned to him and smiled, placing my hand on his chest, his racing heart beating hard against my sweaty palm.

"I'm sorry, sweetie. I sometimes forget not everyone can hear her talk. According to Miss Saffron, that statue on the dresser is a familiar that was accidentally turned into a sleeping cat statue in some sort of witch spell war."

Tyler visibly relaxed and shook his head. "I should have guessed it would have had something to do with magic."

"Madge picked him up at a yard sale nine years ago. It's not a very happy way for a familiar to live out their life."

"You can say that again. Talk about a stuffy, confined existence. I wouldn't wish it on my worst enemy," Miss Saffron muttered, circling the statue one more time.

"We're wasting time. Evelyn. Shadow says he has information about the murder but refuses to share unless you can free him, and we both know you can."

I nodded. "Yes, I can free him."

"Do you think that's wise?" Tyler asked. "I mean, we have no idea if he's dangerous or not."

"Evelyn, trust me. It will all work out," Miss Saffron said. "I've never led you astray before and I'm not about to start now. Imagine if it were me stuck in that statue, you'd want some nice witch to come along and free me, wouldn't you?"

I squeezed Tyler's hand and gave him a peck on his warm cheek. "It's all good, trust me. Okay?"

He paused and his gaze squinted piercing through to my soul.

"Of course, I trust you."

My heart overflowed with love for this man. He pulled my hand up to his lips and planted a kiss on the inside of my palm. A cascade of tingles shot up my arm and lodged in my chest.

"I trust you with my life and my heart."

Whoever said love is overrated has never met my man.

"Earth to Evelyn," Miss Saffron said, a spark of annoyance in her tone. "Time is ticking away. We have a murder to solve, remember?"

I blinked and refocused. "Murder, yes. You're right, we have a murder to solve." I turned and headed towards the dresser. Miss Saffron licked her paw as she sat watching the statue. "Time to get the answers we need."

I placed one hand on the lukewarm sleeping statue and held the other a few inches above its head. I sucked in a deep breath and recited the spell in perfect rhythm. "The gift of life I seek to share, by my hand I do declare. With this spell the change I give, what once was stuck now may live."

A surge of pins and needles bombarded my hands as a shot of pink and silver sparkly swirls swished around my hands and the statue tightly binding them together. My breath caught in my throat as the statue dissolved before my eyes and a black mass of soft, silky fur filled my palm. I snapped my hand back as though it were touching hot coals instead of a furry cat. I rubbed my hands together, alleviating the flow of tingles moving through it.

"Shadow, I presume?"

Tyler stepped up to take the position beside me and the heat from his hand around my waist sent a reassuring jolt through my body. We all watched as the black cat went through every cat stretch known to the world and then turned to me and bowed.

"You truly amaze me, Evelyn." Tyler said, rubbing his hand across my shoulders. "Wait a minute, is he bowing?"

"He sure is." Miss Saffron sat back on her hind legs and licked her paw. "He's grateful to be free from the stationary constraints of that statue."

A lightness filled my chest, and I smiled. "You're welcome. I'm sorry for your loss. You may have been trapped in that statue, but I'm sure you had a fondness for Madge, and now she's gone. You have our sympathies."

Shadow lifted his chin up and then dropped it, acknowledging my words. He looked over at Madge's bed and lowered his gaze once again. The hollow look in his eyes pulled at my own heartstrings.

"I know you're sad, but we don't have a lot of time. I did you a favour, now it's your turn. I know you can only communicate through Miss Saffron, but what can you tell us about the murder? So far, the most we know is that they suspect Nurse Katrina Perez had something to do with it."

The determination and mixture of emotions in Shadow's gaze as he communicated intently with Miss Saffron was something to behold. His paws moved in the same motion that a human's hands did when they were speaking animatedly.

"Well?" I asked.

Miss Saffron's head dipped, and then both cats turned their gazes on Tyler and me. The anticipation was killing me. Miss Saffron licked her lips and ran her paws over her whiskers, then began.

"Shadow is forever grateful to you for releasing him, but he said you have it all wrong. You couldn't be further from the truth."

"Excuse me?" I said, baulking at the audacity of being reprimanded by a cat.

Shadow arched his back and sat on his hind legs, his eyes once again focused on Miss Saffron. I folded my arms across my chest and waited while they continued their discussion, all the while my blood coming to a slow boil.

An unexpectedly sharp meow from Miss Saffron caught my breath. "Okay, don't leave me hanging here. What did he say?"

"Nurse Katrina is innocent," Miss Saffron said, scratching her nails along the emery board on the front of the dresser.

The high-pitched sound resembling nails down a chalkboard. I cringed and shivers goose bumped my skin.

"He said Katrina and Madge may have had their differences, but they always made up in the end and while he can't be 100% sure, Shadow suspects it may have been Gladys."

"Gladys?" The words escaped my lips before my brain kicked into gear. "Why would Gladys kill Madge?"

"Because they were in love with the same man," Miss Saffron said in a perfectly suspicious voice.

I coughed back my shock. "Are you telling me both Gladys and Madge were in love with Arthur?"

Tyler's eyebrows shot up. "No way." His words came out in a gasped whisper as though he was watching a television soapie. "I was not expecting that, but then again, we know all too well jealousy has been known to tear apart a relationship or two."

I pursed my lips and shook my head at the animated expression on Tyler's face. "I'm sure there is more to the story." I turned back to the pair of felines laying comfortably on the top of the dresser side by side. "Okay, spill. I want to know everything. If you saw Gladys kill Madge—"

"He never said he *saw* Gladys kill Madge, only that he suspected," Miss Saffron said, cutting me off mid-sentence.

I rubbed my forehead, trying to smooth out the additional stress lines I was certain were appearing.

"I'm lost. You're going to have to start from the beginning. The abridged version please." I could have sworn I saw Shadow roll his eyes, but I bit my tongue and sucked in a deep breath through my nose.

"Shadow suspects Gladys because being a sleeping statue, he was unable to see what's happening in Madge's room, only hear it. He's been listening in on Madge's conversations for the past nine years. The gossip he could tell you would blow your mind," Miss Saffron said.

"Focus, please," I bit out, staring her down.

"Right." Miss Saffron rubbed her paw over her whiskers and a shudder raced down her spine. "The traffic through the room was quite loud this morning. He heard the door to Madge's room open and close several times, some scuffling, and then a while later, Gladys and Madge in a heated argument about Arthur, and then Gladys was gone."

"Did he hear Madge's voice after Gladys left?" My focus was intently drilling Shadow as his head tilted to the side before he shook it. I wiped my sweaty palms down my thighs and sighed. "Great, this adds a spanner in the works." Turning to Tyler, I gave him my best puppy dog eyes and smiled. I watched his Adam's apple move up and down his neck as he gulped.

"You know I'm putty in your hands when you look at me like that," he said, grimacing and sighing in resignation. "What do you need me to do?"

My chest warmed, and I pushed up and planted a peck on his cheek. "I knew I could count on you. Given this new information, can you give Detective Huxton a call and fill him in and Miss Saffron and I—"

And Shadow. My words interrupted once more by the sweet voice of Miss Saffron shooting through my mind.

I rolled my eyes and sighed. "Miss Saffron, *Shadow* and I will go find Gladys and check out her alibi."

A frown marred his expression. "I'm not keen on you gallivanting off chasing a possible killer, even if it is an elderly woman."

"You're sweet to worry, but I think I've proven on more than one occasion I can take care of myself." I paused and scooped up Miss Saffron from the dresser. Shadow catapulting onto the floor beside my feet. "Besides, not only do I have my trusty furry familiar to help me, but I also now have Shadow. I'm sure he'll help out should the situation arise. Furthermore, what can really go wrong with the place full of visitors?"

Tyler's eyebrows drew together, and he took a small step into my personal space and my stomach dropped.

"I bet that's exactly what Madge thought."

"Madge was not a graduate witch with my growing powers, and my powers are growing all the time. If you'd said to me a year ago that I'd now have the power to heal and slow time just by using my hands and my thoughts, I'd have said you were bonkers. But I can, and with Miss Saffron and Shadow by my side, I'll be fine. Trust me."

The corner of his lips drew up into a half smile. "I know. I guess I've always known you can take care of yourself, but it doesn't stop me from worrying. Maybe I just want to play the hero once in a while."

I spun him around and guided him towards the door. "You will be my hero if you pass the message onto Detective Huxton. We'll try Glady's room first and if she's not there, we'll move into Plan B."

"What's Plan B?" he asked as I shut the door behind us.

I shrugged. "I haven't the foggiest, but I'm sure it will come to me when I need it." After kissing him goodbye, we went in opposite directions.

Please don't make me a liar to my boyfriend.

* * *

My heart raced as I turned the cold metal doorhandle to Gladys' room, my heart racing faster as the seconds ticked over.

"Yoo-hoo, anybody here?" I called, peeking through the door as I slowly eased it open. Not wanting to shock her, I identified myself. "It's Evelyn Grayson. Gladys, are you here? I've brought my therapy cat to meet you." Miss Saffron stamped on my words with her thoughts as soon as the words left my lips.

There you go again with the therapy cat business. Miss Saffron's almond eyes stared up at me. *I tell you, I'm the one that's going to need therapy the way this day is going.*

Ignoring her outburst, I repeated myself. "Gladys, are you here?" The resounding flush of the toilet echoed throughout the room and I paused. Both cats scooted past me and made a beeline for the lounge. Out of the corner of my eye, I saw a large shadowy reflection on the bathroom door as a figure emerged. "Hi Gladys."

She jumped and grabbed her chest, gasping, the wrinkles on her forehead doubling. If that was even possible.

"Evelyn, what are you doing here? You scared me half to death."

I bounded into the room as though nothing was amiss. "I was doing the rounds with my therapy cat and realised I hadn't introduced you two." Miss Saffron stiffened against my arms when I scooped her up from the lounge. I glared down at her and made sure there was no mistaking my intentions this time.

Do you want to find the murderer or not? Go with me on this cat therapy idea. I promise I'll reward you with a huge slice of Aunt Edie's Chocolate Strawberry cake.

A soft purr graced my ears, and she jumped out of my arms and onto the chair beside Gladys and rolled onto her back. That's my girl, sassy and smart.

"Aw look, she wants you to scratch her tummy," I said, smiling, clasping my hands together across my heart. "She must really like you. It's rare she'll do that with someone she barely knows or has never met before. You must be a trustworthy person, Gladys."

I held my breath and glanced at Gladys to see if she reacted to my words. It was only a split-second change, but it was there. Now to go in for the kill. I moved forward and licked my lips.

"This is Miss Saffron. Would you like to pat her or scratch her tummy?"

"Um…" Gladys stood by the chair looking down at Miss Saffron's antics as she rolled around on the chair. Gladys' hand movements were flighty, a true sign of guilt. She let out a quick high-pitch laugh and bit her bottom lip, all the while her gaze never leaving Miss Saffron.

"She only lets those with a kind and honest heart close to her, and that's you. Miss Saffron's a good judge of character, Gladys." I swallowed hard, trying to moisten my dry throat.

"No, no, I can't," she blurted and rushed to sit on her neatly made bed. "That's not me, I'm not a good person." Her hand cupped her mouth, and she squeezed her eyes shut, but a single tear escaped the edge and trickled down her cheek. Her head was shaking from side to side and her shoulders rose and fell with each breath.

Oh gosh, she's going to confess right here.

Her hand dropped to her lap and the spark in her eye I'd seen on previous visits vanished. She crumbled and a sharp pain knotted my chest. Am I really standing in the presence of a murderer?

"I don't understand," I said, bolting over to sit on the chair opposite Gladys. I kept one eye on Gladys, and one eye on the door in case I needed to make a quick exit. "Why aren't you a good person?"

"Because it's my fault Madge is dead." She looked up into my eyes and my gut clenched at the free-flowing tears streaming down her pale, weathered face. "I killed Madge Bromfield."

CHAPTER SIX

The words were like a bomb had exploded inside the room. I looked at the broken woman before me. She'd confessed, but it was a hollow victory.

"I do not believe for one moment this woman killed Madge, and for what it's worth," said Miss Saffron. "And neither does Shadow."

I agree with you.

"Gladys, why on earth would you say that?" I said in my best calming voice. "I don't believe you killed Madge. If you did, you're going to have to explain it to me."

Shadow had stayed in the background since we entered, but even he edged his way forward, wanting to hear her explanation.

"You see." Gladys paused and dabbed the moisture away from her eyes with her pristine white handkerchief. "Madge and I are...were always good friends, but neither of us knew that we'd fallen for the same man until a few months ago."

"Arthur Kingsley?"

She nodded and continued. "Yes. When it came to showing my affection, I was too shy to do anything about it and it took all the courage I had to walk up to him and ask him out. I'd dressed in my best Sunday outfit, put a little rouge on my cheeks. I was headed out to see him only to find Madge had pipped me at the post and asked him out the day before."

"Oh, that must have hurt terribly," I said, the pain embedded in her eyes twisted my stomach in circles.

"It did, and I made Madge pay for it. Every chance I got, I rubbed it in and made her feel as though her happiness was at the cost of mine. I was a terrible friend." Her chin quivered. "But like she said, if Arthur didn't want to date her, he could have said no, but he didn't. He dated her again and again, right in front of me for months. It was torture watching their intimacy grow and then to rub salt in the wound, they got engaged."

I rubbed my forehead and sighed. "You've lost me. I can understand you being a tad jealous, and their engagement must have been hard to take, but explain how it relates to you killing Madge?"

Her head snapped up, and her expression hardened. "I went to her room today and confronted her one last time. She yelled at me and called me raving mad and said that if I did anything to destroy her happiness, she would have me committed to the psychiatric ward. Then she laughed about it. Laughed in my face."

"Do you think she might have been joking?" I asked. "It sounded like a Madge joke to me."

Gladys shook her head vehemently. "No, she was dead serious."

"Then what happened?"

"I was so angry, and my eye caught the framed picture of Arthur sitting on her wall cabinet. I figured that if she was going to have the real thing for the rest of her life, the least she could do was let me have his picture, so I grabbed it. She tried to get it out of my hands, and we struggled. I pushed her, and she fell back against the bathroom door, which gave way, and she tumbled inside. I didn't even stay to see if she was okay. I just turned and bolted. She must have hit her head as she fell."

The sudden bang of the door crashing against the wall had my heart jumping into the back of my throat. Arthur stood in the doorway, his murderous gaze freezing Gladys where she sat.

"How could you?" he said, disdain dripping from each word. "How could you murder the woman I loved, the woman who stole my heart the first moment I saw her?"

Out of the corner of my eye, I saw two bundles of fur brush past me and place themselves defensively between Arthur and Gladys. As a familiar should in defence of an innocent soul. I bolted from my chair, my hands squeezing together to curb the shaking.

"Arthur, how much did you hear of Gladys and my conversation?"

He took a step inside the room, and my back stiffened. "Enough."

This is not how I saw the afternoon playing out. The wrath of a lover scorned was not on today's agenda. I've seen enough disastrous outcomes over the past few years to last me a lifetime. Palm facing him, I held out my hand and slowly lowered it. "I think we all need to calm down."

"Calm down?" His deep voice boomed, and his hands held clenched in fists by his sides. "I will not damn well calm down. That woman took away the love of my life. She can rot in jail for the rest of her life for all I care."

"Who will be rotting in jail?" A perky silver haired woman barked from behind Arthur.

He spun on his heel and glared at the woman. His hand shot out, pointing at Gladys. "She will. Gladys just admitted to killing Madge. I heard her and so did Evelyn."

"What?" The woman's eyebrows shot up into her hairline, exposing the whites of her eyes. She pushed past Arthur and moved to sit by Gladys, placing her arm around Gladys' trembling shoulders. "I don't care what you say. My aunt is not responsible for what happened to Madge, and I'm not just saying that because she's my flesh and blood. I'm saying it because she was with me and the rest of the family at the time of Madge's demise. You can ask any of them.

I'm sure they'll tell you the same thing. We were all out by the therapy ponies. Aunty G had taken a real shine to one of them, so we ended up staying there longer than expected."

My jaw dropped, and a memory snapped back into my mind as though someone switched on a lightbulb.

"Oh my gosh, that's right. I remember she caused a bit of commotion by the ponies and Madge was still alive." A euphoric smile turned the corners of my lips up and I looked at Gladys' confused expression. "You may have argued with Madge and pushed her, but you didn't kill her and if you didn't, that means her killer is still at large."

My words hung in the air as though they were a rain cloud waiting to burst.

"I'm sorry, Arthur." Gladys' shaky voice drifted across the tense silence. "I never meant for you to get hurt. I love…" Her voice trailed off as he stormed from the room. Gladys promptly fell in a heap on the bed in a flood of tears.

"There, there, Aunty G," the woman said, patting her on the back. "I know it has been a rough day, but everything will work out in the end."

Her placating tone grated on my nerves. "Maybe we should go get someone for her to talk to? Maybe see one of the nurses," I suggested.

She waved her hand in the air as though brushing stray wisps of air from her face. She huffed and continued, "Oh, there's no need for that. Aunty G tends to be a bit dramatic these days. I'm sure it will all blow over in a few days."

Gladys shot up off the bed and spun, her gaze glued to her niece as she spoke. "No, no, it won't all blow over in a few days," she bit back, a fresh batch of tears leaking from her eyes as she struggled to speak against her heartache. "The man I love may never speak to me again and one of my dear friends was murdered and all you can do is brush it under the carpet as if it never happened." She paused and ran a hand through her dishevelled hair. "You know what, Lulu? If you can't understand what I'm going through, maybe it's time you stopped visiting all together."

With that, she tossed her hair off her shoulder, turned, and ran from the room. Two furry familiars close on her heels.

Lulu?

I looked at the stern expression on the woman's face. Her pouty pursed lips and wrinkled forehead did not scream Lulu to me. I cleared my throat.

"I'm sure she didn't mean it."

"Oh no, she did. But it's okay. I'm used to it."

Lulu sighed, and her weary smile tightened my chest. She placed a knitted bag on the end of Gladys' bed.

"I only came back to drop off the wool she asked me to get while I was in town the other day. I'll just leave it here." She headed towards the door with her head downcast.

My heart tore in two for the woman. I cringed at the nightmare the woman must go through with each one of Gladys' outbursts. They can't be fun. My heart was instantly full of love and admiration for my Aunt Edie, who still, thank goodness, had all the use of her faculties and brain cells. I bet being a master witch helped in the process.

I called out just as she reached the door, "I'll make sure she gets it."

She paused a moment and glanced over her shoulder. "Thank you." I caught the edge of a grateful smile as she left.

Evelyn, are you coming, or do I have to do all the work around here?

Before I could mull over what just happened with Lulu, Miss Saffron's raspy voice pulled me back to reality.

Yes, I'm coming. Where are you?

"She took us on a wild goose chase, but we've ended up in the laundry, of all places. She's huddled on a stool in the corner. Do you know where it is?"

Yes, I think so. I remember passing it on one of our visits a few months back.

"Hurry, the heat from the clothes dryers is making my coat sticky and wet." She said the final three words with a whimper.

"Poor Miss Saffron," I muttered. Crossing the threshold of Gladys' door, my mind going a hundred miles an hour, I ran straight into a wall of muscle rebounding my entire body back into the room. A strong pair of hands grabbed my waist and pulled me upright against his buff chest, and I gasped. My hands shot to his shoulders for support. The touch so familiar to me I eased my hands across Tyler's trapezius muscles and around his neck and looked into his gorgeous blue eyes.

"Well, if it isn't my hero who saved me from the most catastrophic fall onto the carpet."

"Ha-ha, Evelyn," he grumbled, then smiled. "I'll take any excuse to hold you in my arms."

My gaze fell to his lips and my insides clenched. My breath hitched as his lips closed in on mine.

Evelyn! Where are you? Miss Saffron's screaming voice in my mind shattered the romantic moment, and I jumped back out of his arms.

He frowned. "What's wrong? I thought you liked my kisses. You said they reminded you that there is still beauty in the world."

"I do, but not when Arthur is on the warpath determined to make the person who took his love away pay for their crime. Gladys is off crying in some laundry room being kept company by two cats. One in particular is soaked and grumpy and not to mention there's still a murderer on the loose. That's providing they're still here. Did everything go okay with Detective Huxton?"

He nodded. "Yep, and don't worry about anyone leaving. Detective Huxton has put a temporary hold of visitors leaving until he is sure they're one hundred percent innocent of the crime."

"Good." I grabbed his hand and pulled him along beside me. "I'll explain on the way." I barely had time to update Tyler on what went down in Gladys' room and we were at the laundry door.

"Do you have a neon sign above your head that reads, 'Danger, come find me' or something?" he asked, folding his arms across his chest pushing his pecs right up into my eyeline.

I drew my gaze away and jerked my head back. "Pfft, don't be silly." I turned the warm metal doorhandle and cracked the door. A whoosh of hot air exploded in my face and I sucked in an unexpected breath and spluttered all over the place. "Yuk, that's disgusting. Remind me never to get a clothes dryer as long as I live."

"You got it," he said with a sly smirk.

Gladys sat in a defeated huddle on a stool in the corner, her head bowed, her arms wrapped tightly around her waist in a protective gesture. Who could blame her? Not me. Even though the temperature was soaring, a shiver ran down my spine and lodged itself in my nauseas gut.

I whispered in Tyler's direction, "Might be better if you stay here. She wasn't the best when she ran out and I'd hate her to close up when she sees you."

He nodded, and I moved off. Grabbing a stool, I perched my backside on it a few feet from Gladys and waited a moment until she sensed my presence. Miss Saffron and Shadow stood off to the side, both looking like they'd been through the washer and came out before the spin cycle had started. I bit my lip, holding my laughter at bay.

"I'm sorry, Evelyn." Gladys' soft mutter drew my attention away from my familiar. "I had no idea I was causing so much fuss today."

"Don't be sorry. We can't help who we fall in love with, right?" I felt Tyler's eyes igniting me from the inside out. I chanced a quick glance his way and was rewarded with a nod and a brimming smile. "It was an accident."

"I...no..." She shook her head and rubbed her hands down her thighs as though trying to dry them. "I was so blindsided with my love for Arthur, I think I've made a terrible mistake."

Mistake?

"What do you mean 'mistake'?" My muscles tensed.

"You see, I was protecting him. I could never let anything happen to him. That's why I confessed to killing Madge. I couldn't let him be blamed for her murder."

My stomach fluttered while Gladys' words were a jumbled mess in my mind as I tried to make heads or tails of them. "But Gladys, you said you and Madge fought over Arthur's picture and you accidentally pushed her. She fell against the bathroom door and then you left. Are you telling me you lied?"

She slowly nodded. Sweat beaded her brow, but that could be from the heat radiating off the clothes dryers, couldn't it? I looked at Tyler and he circled his hand as though to say keep going. After a curt nod in his direction, I turned back to Gladys.

"I think it would be best if you started from the beginning, so we're both on the same page and this time, stick to the truth." My reprimanding tone was enough that Gladys' back straightened, and she swallowed hard before nodding.

"Madge was one of my closest friends here at Noble Crest, and even though I was in love with Arthur, I knew he'd made his choice, and it wasn't me. It broke my heart every day, but somewhere deep down I was happy for them." She paused and licked her lips.

"Go on."

"I heard someone had killed Madge, but I didn't believe it, so I snuck away from my family and went to see for myself."

"Wait a minute." I held up my hand. "They practically blocked off all the entrances to her room. How did you get past?"

"I know more secret passages in this place than you can count on two hands." Her empty gaze seemed to dissolve as she spoke. "This place was an old hospital years ago before you arrived in town. All the renovations they made to it hid its haunted past, but they couldn't hide the secret tunnels and hidey places in the walls."

"You mean to tell me that this place was renovated to look like a resort and it was all done to cover up its history?"

She nodded and grinned. "I'm sure it wasn't on purpose. They were renovating to create this place."

"Evelyn, can we please get back to the murder before I turn into a ball of wet fur permanently?" Miss Saffron grunted.

I cringed and looked over at both Miss Saffron and Shadow. They looked like someone doused them with a garden hose.

I continued. "They'll be plenty of time to talk about this place later, and we will talk, but right now can you get back to the part where you went to see for yourself if Madge was dead."

Gladys' lips thinned, and she gave a quick nod. "Right, so when I got there, I stepped inside her door and my entire body froze when I saw her laying on the tiles of her bathroom, a pool of blood near her head. I wanted to see her one last time, but I couldn't. My stomach doesn't deal with the sight of blood at the best of times. I turned to leave, but what friend would I be if I didn't see if they'd taken anything else other than her life? At first, it looked as if nothing had been moved and then I saw it."

My fingers fidgeted wildly with each other. I pushed my palms onto my knees and leaned in closer.

"What did you see, Gladys?"

"I wasn't sure at first." Her twitchy hand moved into her pocket, and she withdrew something and held it tight in her palm. "It was on the floor just outside the bathroom, masked by a section of broken skirting board. A badge. I recognised it cause my dad had one similar. He got his in the army and I remember Arthur served in the army, so I figured it must have been his. I picked it up to return it to him and…" She squeezed her lips and eyes together and sucked in a deep breath.

"And?" I prodded.

"And there was blood on the pin and back of the badge and it dawned on me it must have been Madge's or Arthur's blood. It must have come off in a struggle. I know you won't understand, but I love him, and I couldn't let him go to jail. I just couldn't. So I took it and hid it in my pocket. I'd do anything to protect the man I love. Surely you can understand that?"

More than you'll ever know.

My pulse raced, and Tyler's rigid body standing by the doorway drew my gaze. His intense stare spoke to my soul. Yes, I'd go to the ends of the world to protect the man I love, this man. I smiled softly at him and then turned back to Gladys, breathing steadily even though my pounding heart was beating crazily fast inside my ribcage.

"Gladys, can I have a look at the badge, please?"

A moment of uncertainty coated her expression, and then her fingers slowly opened. My heart practically stopped inside my chest when I saw the shining pin sitting in her palm. My jaw dropped, and I couldn't take my eyes off the acronym in bold letters on the front of the badge. I knew it, or at least I'd heard of it. In fact, I'd heard it mentioned earlier today.

"That is no war badge, Gladys," I said, my words coming fast.

Her brows drew together, and she looked down at her palm. "What do you mean?"

"That image there," I pointed just under the words, "is a rolling pin like you use to roll pastry and those big initials read M.O.D. Do you know what they stand for?"

She shook her head. "No, do you?"

"I'm afraid I do. M.O.D stands for Master of Desserts and I know someone who owns one, or at least he did earlier today. Nigel Blakely."

CHAPTER SEVEN

"Nigel? Are you sure?"

"I'm afraid so. Sasha was only telling me this morning how he's won all these awards and then mentioned the exact pin you're holding in your hand. It can't be a coincidence. I'm sure there aren't too many M.O.D members that visit Noble Crest. I can't help thinking Nigel and this badge had something to do with Madge's death. After all, Madge would have been his new mother-in-law once she and Arthur married."

I grabbed Gladys' hand, giving it a reassuring squeeze. "Arthur may have had nothing to do with the murder. He could be innocent. Wouldn't that be good?"

A brimming smile crept across Gladys' face and it was the first time since the murder a spark of hope ignited in my belly.

"Oh yes, that would be good. At least I can clear his name, and in time, hopefully I can explain to him my part in this horrid affair."

"We can run through all sorts of scenarios, but we're going to be no closer to finding out the truth unless we go straight to the source," Miss Saffron said. "And get out of this infernal heat box at the same time."

"Agreed." I bolted from my chair, my body renewed with energy. "Time to find Nigel. Who's with me?" Cheers, yeses, and a crescendo of meows filled the room. "Right, Gladys, you come with me and we'll start looking inside. Miss Saffron and Shadow, you go with Tyler and take the outside. If either of us finds him, we call the other person before approaching him. If you luck out, we'll meet back at the main reception in twenty minutes."

* * *

I checked my watch and sure enough, twenty minutes had passed. Gladys and I had come up empty-handed. We'd flitted around, avoiding anyone who looked suspicious enough and likely to question us. We headed for the main reception desk, my head throbbing while my churning guts was bordering on a full-blown nausea attack.

"I don't get it," I said to Gladys, pinching the bridge of my nose. "It's going to be time for the Easter Bonnet Parade soon, which is the final event of the day and then everyone will want to leave, including Nigel, if he hasn't already. Let's hope Tyler has had more luck."

"Maybe I should check on Arthur?" Gladys said, more as a passing comment than a question.

The longing in her gaze put a lump in the back of my throat.

"He may not forgive me, but I must know he is all right."

I nodded and patted her forearm. "I think that's a brilliant idea. I'll meet Tyler at reception and fill him in and you go check in on Arthur." She threw her arms around my shoulders and squeezed, and then she was off.

As I turned the corner, I saw Tyler standing at the reception desk chatting with Isla. I paused and took in her flirty laugh and battering eyelids, and my heart sank for all the wrong reasons. Even though she had helped me out earlier, Isla was a naturally flirty woman, and it didn't stop my jealous streak from making an unexpected appearance where Tyler was concerned. I pulled up behind him and cleared my throat and he spun; the colour draining from his face.

Isla looked up and gasped. A glow of cherry-red washed up her cheeks, clashing with the fire-engine red hue of her hair.

"Evelyn, I didn't see you there."
Obviously not.

"Tyler and I were just talking about the success of the day and how so many families had turned up to support the event. He's been so supportive of Jeffrey.

I was congratulating him on their win in the three-legged race."

The woman's words blurted out one after the other in quick succession, as though she thought I was going to rip into her. In the deep recesses of my belly, the thought may have crossed my mind, but that's for couples with trust issues, and I trusted Tyler unconditionally. I softened my smile.

"It sure has been a successful day, except for maybe the Madge being murdered part."

Her face fell. "Oh yeah, there was that."

I threaded my arm through Tyler's and gifted her one of my big 'everything-is-going-to-be-okay' smiles.

"Would you excuse us for a moment?" I pulled Tyler to the side, out of earshot of the red-headed beauty. "I'm guessing you didn't have much luck finding Nigel either?"

He shook his head. "Nope. We combed the outside pretty good and still came up empty handed and somehow I lost Miss Saffron and Shadow on the way."

I rubbed the back of my neck, the skin on my hand heating on contact. "I think we're going to have to call Detective Huxton in to help and..." My words slipped away into the oblivion, startled by the sound of Sasha's voice behind me talking to Isla. If anyone knew where Nigel was, surely it would be his wife?

"Sasha, hi," I said, scooting over beside her. "It's been a pretty full-on day, hasn't it?"

She sighed, rubbing her stomach. "Sure has. I'm exhausted, not to mention stuffed, after eating so much of the good food provided today."

"I know what you mean. My waistline expanded just looking at all that food." A pretend giggle escaped my lips, and I ignored Tyler's eye roll. "Tyler and I were looking for Nigel. I don't suppose you know where he is?"

She huffed. "Sure do. We were doing the rounds saying our goodbyes, and he informed me he had to go to the toilet. He came up to use the guest toilet at reception. That's why I came in. He's been gone a while now, so I came looking for him."

"Um, excuse me," Isla said, politely interrupting. "I couldn't help overhearing. As far as I know, Nigel hasn't used the guest toilet. He did mention he'd left his jacket in one of the rooms and that you'd lost your key card to get in, so I made him another one."

Sasha frowned and fished out a plastic card from her pocket. "You mean this card? Nigel knew I had the card."

"How strange. If he knew you had the card, why would he want another one? Why not just ask you for it?" Isla asked. I could see the clogs ticking over in her head.

Why indeed?

"Wait, did you say he came looking for his jacket?" Sasha asked a confused Isla. She nodded. "That doesn't make any sense. His jacket is with our bags and empty Crème Brûlée containers, but he knew that all along. He was the one who put it there in the first place."

The blood in my veins turned to ice. Why lie unless you have something to hide or cover up, like a murder?

Sasha's questioning gaze looked at each of us in turn. "Which means if he wasn't looking for his jacket or going to the toilet, what was he doing up here?"

"That's the million-dollar question," Tyler said.

My chest tightened, and I pushed the nagging feeling from my thoughts. It was my heart that convinced me I'd found Madge's murderer. There's one place we haven't looked for him…the scene of the crime.

"I have a theory and if you'll indulge me a moment, I'd like to see if I'm right." I waited for Sasha's nod of approval and then looked at Isla. "Can you please call Detective Huxton? I know he's still on the premises and ask him to meet us at Madge's room."

She frowned, giving her one nasty monobrow. "Why?"

"Because if I'm right." *And I know I am.* "That's where the murderer will be. Can you do that for me, Isla?"

She nodded and picked up the phone receiver, her eyes wide, the whites of her eyes staring straight back at me. An electric buzz heightened my senses and a fluttery rolling wave stirred in the empty recesses of my stomach. Sasha stood staring at me and I swallowed, then I let out a semi-frantic giggle.

Sasha folded her arms across her chest and tilted her head, her stern gaze an indication of what was to come.

"What is going on, Evelyn? You are acting strangely, calling Detective Huxton to meet you at Madge's room, and what is this theory of yours?"

I turned and headed off, calling over my shoulder as both Tyler and Sasha followed me. "At the moment it's just a theory, but don't you think it's odd that Tyler, Gladys, me, or you cannot find Nigel?"

Sasha stopped dead in her tracks, her hands on her hips, lips flattened and her eyes narrowing.

"Are you telling me you think Nigel had something to do with Madge's murder?"

My lips parted at her accusatory tone. Tyler stepped up beside me and the supportive warmth from his body spurred me on.

"Yes, that's exactly what I am saying."

"That's ridiculous." Sasha huffed. "Nigel loved Madge and vice versa. He was fully supportive of my dad marrying Madge. In fact, he was to make their wedding cake."

"That may be so, but all the pieces add up."

"What pieces?" Sasha snapped through clenched teeth.

"There's many, but one in particular."

I reached into my pocket and pulled out the M.O.D badge. It was as though I'd picked up a burning hot coal in my bare hand. I opened my clenched fist in front of her and she gasped. Sasha's hand flattened against her sternum and her wide-eyed gaze glued to the badge in my hand.

"Gladys found this on the floor in Madge's room and the only way it could have got there is if Nigel had been in her room. You mentioned earlier that he was a member of M.O.D and had the badge to prove it. I'm guessing this is his badge."

Tyler piped up beside me. "And if you look closely enough, the clasp is bent, so it didn't just fall off and that's blood. The question is, whose blood?"

I brought the badge up and examined it. "Does it look familiar?"

Sasha paled, then nodded. "It looks like Nigel's but there's no way to be 100% sure, besides, it's missing the rest of it."

Her words hit me square in the chest, and the air drained from my lungs. "What do you mean 'the rest of it?'"

"Well, if it's Nigel's, there should be an extra bit attached to the bottom that reads, *Five Years*. It's missing, or you've made a mistake and it belongs to someone else."

Am I missing something here? Can the woman really be that much in denial?

My whole body tensed, and my chest felt as tight as an elastic band, ready to snap.

"I think it's a very slim chance there would be another Master of Desserts here at Noble Crest the same day as Nigel, don't you?"

Tyler spoke the exact words rolling around in my mind. He stepped out from behind me, his buff chest puffed out, and he sucked in a lungful of air.

"I'm betting the reason we can't find Nigel is because he's searching for his badge or the missing part right now."

I turned to Tyler and snapped my fingers, my mind as clear as the sky on a cool spring afternoon. "That's right and hypothetically, if Nigel did kill Madge, her room would be where he'd start looking for the missing piece to his badge. Right?" I turned and headed for the door, my key card connecting with the keypad long enough to open it, and I was off, weaving my way through the lonely corridors towards Madge's room. Mutters and mumbles graced my ears as Tyler and Sasha made haste to keep up with me.

"Wait up Evelyn," Tyler called. "Hadn't we better wait for Detective Huxton?"

"No need, I'm here." The stately figure of the police detective pulled up in front of us, seemingly out of nowhere.

The deep timbre of Detective Huxton's voice caught me off guard. "Where did you come from?"

"I've been around. Care to fill me in on what's going on?"

Adrenaline spiked my pulse into overdrive, and I continued my trek double time to Madge's room, Detective Huxton joining my entourage.

"Tyler and I believe Nigel had something to do with Madge's death."

"Which is preposterous, of course," Sasha spat, her arms pumping to keep pace. "My husband is not a killer."

We turned the corner, and a startled high-pitch screech bellowed from Madge's room. Detective Huxton's arm shot out in front of me like an iron bar slamming into my chest. Pain ricocheted down my sternum, past my belly, and into my legs.

"Ow."

His revolver drawn, he mouthed, "Wait here."

And let you have all the fun? Not likely.

I edged my feet forward to follow closely on his tail and in one almighty pull, Tyler yanked me backwards straight into his wall of muscly chest.

"Sorry, but you'll thank me later," he whispered in my ear.

His hot breath skimmed my sensitive skin beneath my earlobe, sending goose bumps spreading over my neck. My gaze dropped to his hand, planted securely around mine.

"I'm not about to let you walk into a room with a potential murderer when there's a perfectly good detective with a gun ready to take down whoever is in there. No need to risk your life."

The silence shattered by a torrent of screeching meows and hisses. My heart jumped into my throat.

"Miss Saffron?" With Tyler's attention distracted by the same sound, I wrangled my hand free and high-tailed it to Madge's room, pulling up next to Detective Huxton. The sight before me re-energised my spirits, and I fist-pumped the air. My gaze locked on the cowering face of Nigel recoiling in the corner of the room, his wide eyes staring at Gladys, fear coating his pale expression.

"Gladys, no."

Tyler's soft voice startled me. My gaze shot up and my pulse raced at the image of Gladys pointing a kitchen knife at Nigel, her murderous gaze sending a shot of ice through my veins.

"Gladys, what are you doing?" I asked, an invisible hand squeezing the air from my windpipe.

She shunted towards Nigel and my heart just about stopped.

"He killed Madge and tried to blame Arthur. He deserves the same as far as I'm concerned."

Detective Huxton eased himself further inside the room, his vacated spot taken by Sasha. The pained stare on her face clawed at my heart.

"Nigel? What did you do?"

Nigel held his hands up, blocking his body from Gladys' onslaught. "I…I didn't do anything."

"Liar," Gladys hissed, shunting her arm forward. The light beamed off the tip of the silver blade, sending a rainbow of colours scattering across the wall. "Tell the truth. Tell them why you killed Madge."

Sasha grabbed the doorframe, steadying her swaying body. "What is she talking about, Nigel?"

Both Miss Saffron and Shadow stood by Gladys' side, their ears standing straight up and their stances frozen. Nigel attempted to stand, and both cats dropped to the ground. A guttural hiss escaped as they started a low crawl towards their prey.

Miss Saffron…no. Don't do anything you'll regret.

"Give me some credit. I'm not about to throw my life away on this pathetic excuse for a human being, but can't a cat have a little fun once in a while?" she hissed.

My chest eased at her playful banter, but it was the sight of Gladys' shaking hand that still had my pulse racing. Time to wrap this up. I cleared my throat and held up the M.O.D badge in full view of everyone, especially Nigel.

"Tell me, are you looking for this?"

Nigel's jaw dropped as his gaze landed on the badge. "What…how…" His shoulders heaved up and down, his eyes never leaving the badge. "I have no idea what that is."

Sasha gasped beside me, and her lips thinned. "Don't lie, Nigel. You know exactly what that is. After all, it's yours, isn't it?"

Nigel tugged at his collar, and his gaze dropped, a crimson blush bleeding through his cheeks.

"Look at me, Nigel," Sasha barked. "Tell the damn truth. Is this your badge?"

Nigel's chest deflated before my eyes as though someone had let the air out of his body. His head lowered, and his lips locked together.

"It looks like we're at a stand-off," Detective Huxton muttered. He lowered his gun slightly and glanced at the knife. "Gladys, how about you give me that knife? It's not like he can go anywhere. Evelyn, Tyler, and Sasha have blocked the door, so there's no escape. I'm not about to let him get away. If he tries, I'll shoot him. Sound fair?"

Gladys stood her ground, her intense fevered stare sending shivers up my spine. She stiffened, and then the air whooshed from her lungs in one enormous breath. She smiled and lowered her arm, holding the knife out towards Detective Huxton, handle first.

"Glad I could be of assistance. I wasn't really going to hurt him. After what he did to Madge, I just wanted to make him squirm for a while."

Whoa.

My head spun with giddiness, and my shoulders dropped. Even I believed Gladys.

"What about the missing piece of the badge?" I asked. Nigel's chin lifted, and he pulled at the skin on his neck. A nervous worry gesture if I ever saw one.

"We don't need it," Detective Huxton said, placing the knife on the cabinet as far away from everyone as possible. "Although I expect that's why Nigel is in here, to find it. Am I right, Nigel?"

All eyes turned to the man still cowering in the corner of the room, his eyebrows drawn together. He opened his mouth to speak and closed it just as quick.

Detective Huxton continued. "It makes no difference if you talk or not, Nigel. You see, I'm a Leodian and do you know what powers a Leodian has?"

Nigel sat frozen like a marble statue, a small shake of his head the only indication he was still breathing.

"A Leodian has the power to hold an object in their hand and see its past."

He pointed to my hand.

"Take that badge, for instance. Once I pick it up, I'll be able to see its past and what happened to it and how it ended up in Evelyn's hand. What do you think it's going to show me, Nigel?"

The blood drained from his face as Detective Huxton's words sunk in. "I...you..."

"I'll let you in on a little secret," Detective Huxton continued, crouching down to Nigel's eye level. "If I have to use my powers to find out who owns that badge and what it had to do with Madge's murder, the consequences for the guilty party are going to be far greater than if they own up of their own volition."

The tension in the air was growing thicker by the second.

"Have it your way," Detective Huxton said, rising and turning towards me.

"Okay, you win. It was me." Nigel's defeated voice broke through the stale silence.

Audible gasps were heard all round. "What was you? You're going to have to say it out loud, Nigel."

Nigel's back stiffened, and he pinned his arms across his stomach. "I killed Madge Bromfield."

Sasha's hand flew to cover her gaping mouth. Tears trickled down her cheeks, and she shook her head.

"No, no, no, this can't be happening. Why Nigel? For heaven's sakes, why?"

"Like you would understand," he spat the disdainful words at his wife like she was a speck of dirt beneath his shoe.

"What?" she said, her eyes dulling beside her pasty complexion. "What wouldn't I understand?"

"It's always been easy for you. You've always had money. Your dad's loaded."

"Is that why you married me?" she asked behind gritted teeth. "For my dad's money?"

"Not at first. I did love you, but it was clear that the only way I was going to get my own pastry house was with the family money." Nigel eased himself up off the floor but stayed locked against the wall. "I had full intentions of going into partnership with Arthur, and then you put him in Noble Crest. I knew it was only a matter of time before he wasted away, and his inheritance would fall into your hands."

"Go on," Detective Huxton said, urging him to continue.

Nigel rubbed the creases on his forehead. "I'd made promises I couldn't keep, committed to deals that I needed to make payments for. I was in deep and the only way out I could see was with Arthur's money. He was interested in a partnership. Until he fell in love with Madge. His focus changed. The only partnership he wanted was with Madge, travelling the world and living the rest of their lives in luxury here at Noble Crest."

"And you couldn't stand to see him happy, could you?" Sasha stood, tremors shooting through her hands. She clenched them into fists at her sides, and it was clear she was struggling to hold it together.

Nigel's skin flushed, and his nostrils flared. "And what about me? I'm a Master pastry chef. Don't I deserve to be happy? I've worked hard all my life, and it was all on target until Madge came on the scene. I spoke with her this morning and tried to get her to back off. Break up with Arthur just until I could get him to commit to the partnership, but she wouldn't have it. She stormed off, vowing to tell him everything and then all would be lost."

"So, you had to stop her?" I asked, while he was still confessing.

"Darn tootin' I did." His body shook, and Detective Huxton took a step forward and slowly pushed Gladys behind him. Nigel continued, oblivious to his movements. "She was going to expose me, a double blow. First, losing Arthur as a partner, and then exposing me. I would have lost everything. Nah, that wasn't an option. I gave it one last chance to talk to her, to make her understand my point of view. I paid her a visit here."

He paused, and the blood drained from his cheeks. His gaze turned towards the bathroom where her body was found, and his shoulders slumped.

"I never meant to kill her. I just wanted to talk, to make her understand what was at stake. And then we got into an argument and before I knew it, we were struggling. I pushed her away, and she ripped my badge from my jacket in the struggle. She fell back into the door and smashed her head on the handle and then the floor. It was an accident really."

"Accident or not, I'll not stay married to someone who would put money over the happiness of others." Tears trickled down Sasha's damp cheeks and she wiped them away with the back of her palm.

Nigel flinched at her words. He reached out towards her, and when she pulled back, his hands dropped in defeat.

"My dad loved you and was only ever supportive of your career, and you repay him by killing his fiancée? I can't even stand to look at you, let alone breathe the same air. We're done. I'm hiring the best divorce lawyer I can find and believe me when I say I will make you pay for what you have done."

I jumped as she turned on her heel, her hair slashing across my face as she flicked her head and stormed off.

"Ow," I muttered, rubbing my cheek where it had made contact.

"I think we can continue this down at the station," Huxton said, as he expertly handcuffed a deflated Nigel. "Excuse us, Evelyn...Tyler."

I blew the air out of my lungs, stepped back and sagged against Tyler's hardened wall of muscle, his arms enveloping me in a comforting embrace. He leaned down and whispered, his warm breath tickling the sensitive skin behind my ear.

"Congratulations, you were right. Detective Huxton was lucky you were on the case. Although, I did not see that one coming. I mean about Nigel wanting Arthur's inheritance to open a pastry shop."

I stood with Tyler's arms securely wrapped around me, watching Nigel's head hang low as the detective led him away.

"Yeah, me neither. I guess an obsession with money that strong could push someone over the edge."

A bellowing foghorn blared from the direction of the outdoor area, and I cringed, covering my ears.

"What is that awful sound?"

Gladys gasped, and her jaw dropped. "Oh no, we're going to miss it."

Her squealing tone had the ends of my hair standing on end, sending goose bumps racing down my spine. "Going to miss what?"

"The Easter Bonnet Parade, silly. It's the last event of the day. So many of the patients have made their own bonnets this year. And if anything can cheer us up, it's an Easter Bonnet Parade." She bent down and opened her arms and within seconds, two furry familiars snuggled under her chin. "I can't leave these two gorgeous cats behind. If it wasn't for their support, I may never have had the courage to confront Nigel in the first place. I'm going to get each of them an extra special sugary treat."

Gladys sailed past.

"There may be something in this cat therapy idea of yours after all, Evelyn," Miss Saffron said in her typical cheeky tone, followed by a sassy chuckle.

"Are you kidding me?" I folded my arms across my chest and watched, mystified as Shadow and my trusty familiar, the traitor that she was, burrowed down in Gladys' arms as she tickled her under her chin.

"Come on," Tyler said, grabbing my hand. "I promised Jeffrey I'd walk with him in the parade."

"Sure." I chuckled and walked double time to keep up with Tyler's stride. What a way to end the day. A puzzle solved, a murderer caught, a new familiar friend and an Easter Bonnet Parade fit for a king. I glanced at Tyler and warm fuzzies scooted through my belly.

Not a king exactly, but a God, my Greek God-looking boyfriend.

Who could ask for anything more?

THE END

Connect with Polly

You can sign up for my newsletter here:
Polly Holmes Newsletter

Keep up to date on Polly's book releases, signings
and events on her website:
Polly Holmes Website

Follow her on her Facebook page:
Polly Holmes Facebook Page

Check out all the latest news in her Facebook group:
Danger, Mystery, Romance: Polly Holmes Facebook
Group

Follow her on her Instagram page:
https://www.instagram.com/plharris_pollyholmes_
author/

Follow her on Bookbub:
https://www.bookbub.com/authors/polly-holmes

Thank you for reading
Cats, Crime and Crème Brûlée
If you enjoyed this story, why not start reading
Evelyn's adventures from the series from the
beginning. Turn the page to see where it all started.

Buy links for Pumpkin Pies & Potions #1

Amazon US
Amazon AU
Amazon UK
Amazon CA

Witches, cats, pumpkin pies and murder!

I'm Evelyn Grayson and if you'd told me by the time I was 23, I'd have lost both my parents in a mysterious accident, moved in with the coolest Aunt ever, lived in a magical town, and I was a witch, I would have said you were crazy. Funny thing is, you'd be right.

Camille Stenson, the grumpiest woman in Saltwater Cove is set on making this year's Halloween celebrations difficult for everyone, but when she turns up dead and my best friend is on the suspect list, I have no choice but to find out whodunit and clear her name.

Amongst the pumpkin carving, abandoned houses, and apple bobbing, it soon becomes apparent dark magic is at play and I must use all my newfound witches' abilities to find the killer before another spell is cast.

Step into Evelyn Grayson's magical world in the first book of the Melting Pot Café series, a fun and flirty romantic paranormal cozy mystery where the spells are flowing, and the adventure is just beginning.

Buy links for Happy Deadly New Year #2

Amazon US
Amazon AU
Amazon UK
Amazon CA

Never in my lifetime did I think I'd spend New Year's Eve knee-deep in mischief, magic, and murder!

When my high-school nemesis, Prudence McAvoy, chooses The Melting Pot Café to host her New Year's party, I know I'm courting trouble by accepting her booking. The trouble begins with Prudence turning up dead, face down in a pond, and the finger for her murder is pointed directly at my shape-shifting best friend, Jordi.

Determined to clear Jordi's name and bring the real killer to justice, I pool resources with Harriet, Tyler, and my cheeky familiar, Miss Saffron, to find out what happened to Prudence. As the clock counts down to midnight, time is running out in more ways than one.

Can we find the killer before another body drops? Or will Jordi's new year begin in the pokey?

Buy links for Muffins & Magic #3

Amazon US
Amazon AU
Amazon UK
Amazon CA

What's a witch to do when faced with protecting the ones she loves against an unimaginable evil?

Ever had one of those days when everything is going too well? When you have that sense that the other boot is about to drop? Welcome to my day.

It's the Annual Saltwater Cove Show, and this year there are more rides, show bags, food stalls, and competitions than ever before. Witches from worlds near and far have descended to try their hand at winning the prestigious Witch Wonder Trophy for best witch baker.

When Seraphina Morgan from the Coven of the Night Moon turns up dead, all avenues lead to last year's reigning champion, Aunt Edie, as the guilty party. Dark magic is lurking, and I'm determined to get to the bottom of it and clear Aunt Edie's name before the unthinkable happens, and she's found guilty. Enlisting the help of my two best friends and drop-dead greek-god gorgeous boyfriend, we set about finding the real killer before Aunt Edie's goose is cooked. Or pie is baked as the case may be.

BUY LINKS FOR MISTLETOE, MURDER & MAYHEM #4

Amazon US
Amazon AU
Amazon UK
Amazon CA

Christmas is Saltwater Cove's favourite holiday of the year, but that didn't stop murder and mayhem from making an unscheduled visit.

The festive spirit is out and about, the eggnog is flowing, mistletoe is hung, and the town is pumped for the most exciting event on the Christmas calendar, the Annual Concert. This year aunt Edie decided it would be a brilliant idea to volunteer me and my best friend, Harriet, to run both Santa's photo booth *and* the refreshment stall.

As the celebrations kick-off, things turn complicated fast when my childhood friend, Trixie Snowball, winner of the Elf of the Year contest, reveals she's lost Santa's list and is desperate to find it. I agreed to use my magic to help, but things take a turn for the worse when the runner-up of the contest turns up dead behind the refreshment stall, and Trixie is the number one suspect.

Christmas day is fast approaching, and now I'm in a race against time to find a murderer, clear Trixie's name, bring the real killer to justice and find the list before disappointment rains down on children all over the world. How, oh, how did I get myself into such a predicament?

Buy links for A Deadly Disappearance Down Under #5

Amazon US
Amazon AU
Amazon UK
Amazon CA

Solving the disappearance of my best friends' parents was NOT one of my New Year's Resolutions…

A trip to sunny Australia in the scorching summer wasn't in my holiday plans, but when Jordi rings in a state of utter panic revealing her parents failed to turn up at the annual Shapeshifters Conference held in country Western Australia, what's a girl to do?

Despite having solved a murder or two in my time, I am completely out of my comfort zone in the harsh Aussie outback where not only the sun, insects, and snakes bite, but the locals do too.

The search is interrupted when the body of Harridan Reef local and chairman of the Shapeshifters Executive Council, Shayla Ramos, turns up dead in a sheep paddock at the local country show. I'm convinced her murder is linked to Jordi's missing parents. But what if I'm wrong?

Forbidden to use magical powers in a town where the supernatural is concealed from view, it becomes apparent the locals have their own secrets. Secrets someone is willing to kill to keep hidden.

Together with Aunt Edie, Detective Huxton Harriet, Jordi, Tyler and my trusty furry familiar, Miss Saffron, we must all work together to uncover the truth. With a blazing bush fire threatening to destroy all in its path we must race the clock to unlock the secrets before Jordi's parents pay the ultimate price.

Thank you for reading
Cats, Crime and Crème Brûlée
If you enjoyed this story, I would really appreciate it
if you would consider leaving a review of this book,
no matter how short, at the retailer site where you
bought your copy or on sites like Goodreads.

YOU are the key to this book's success and the
success of **The Melting Pot Café Cozy Mystery
Series.** I read every review and they really do make
a huge difference.

ABOUT THE AUTHOR

Polly Holmes is the cheeky, sassy alter ego of Amazon best-selling author, *P.L. Harris*. When she's not writing her next romantic suspense novel as *P.L. Harris*, she is planning the next murder in one of Polly's cozy mysteries. She pens food-themed and paranormal cozy mysteries and publishes her books solely with Gumnut Press.

As *Polly Holmes*, *Cupcakes and Corpses* was a finalist in the Oklahoma Romance Writers of America's <u>2019 IDA International Digital Awards,</u> short suspense category. *Cupcakes and Curses* claimed second place and *Cupcakes and Cyanide* gained third place making it a clean sweep in the category.

She won silver in the <u>2020 ROAR! National Business Awards</u> in the *Writer/Blogger/Author* category and for the second year in a row, she was a finalist in the <u>2021 ROAR! National Business Awards</u> winning bronze in the *Writer/Blogger/Author* category with Gumnut Press taking out the gold in the *Hustle and Heart* category.

Muffins & Magic and *Mistletoe, Murder & Mayhem* was long-listed in the 2022 Davitt Awards, a prestigious award run by the Sisters of Crime, Australia. *Muffins & Magic* also received second place in the 2022 MMH—Making Magic Happen Book Awards. She has also been nominated for the 2022 Mumpreneur Awards. *Muffins & Magic* was also a finalist in the 2022 Killer Nashville Silver Falchion Awards.

When she's not writing you can find her sipping coffee in her favourite cafe, watching reruns of Murder, She Wrote or Psych, or taking long walks along the beach soaking up the fresh salty air.

READ ON FOR AN EXCERPT OF #1

PUMPKIN PIES & POTIONS.

CHAPTER ONE

"Oh, my goodness, breakfast smells divine," I said, bounding down the stairs two at a time toward the lip-smacking scent streaming from the kitchen. Rubbing my grumbling stomach, I peeked over Aunt Edie's shoulder at the green gooey concoction boiling on the stove. I've been living with my aunt for the past eleven years since my parents died, and not once have I questioned her cooking abilities. Until now. I folded my arms and leant against the kitchen bench. "I know it smells amazing but are you sure it's edible because it sure as heck doesn't look like it."

Aunt Edie frowned and her eyebrows pulled together. Her classic pondering expression. She snapped her fingers and looked straight at me with her golden honey-brown eyes glowing like she'd just solved the world's climate crisis.

"Popcorn. I forgot the popcorn. Evelyn, honey be a dear and grab me the popcorn from the second shelf in the pantry. The caramel packet, not the plain."

Caramel popcorn for breakfast? That's a new one.

I shrugged. "Sure." Walking into Aunt Edie's pantry was like walking into the potions classroom at Hogwarts. Every witch's dream pantry. Normal food on the left-hand side and on the right, every potion ingredient a witch could possibly need, clearly labelled in its allocated spot. Aunt Edie would always say: a place for everything and everything in its place.

"I can't believe Halloween is only three days away," I called, swiping the caramel popcorn bag off the shelf. Heading back out, the hunger monster growing in my stomach grumbled, clearly protesting the fact I still hadn't satisfied its demand for food.

Aunt Edie's cheeks glowed at the mention of the annual holiday. "I know. It's my most favourite day of the year, aside from Christmas, that is."

"Of course." I handed her the bag of popcorn and made a beeline for the coffee machine. My blood begged to be infused with caffeine. Within minutes, I held a steaming cup of heaven in my hands. As I sipped, the hot liquid danced down my throat in euphoric bliss.

"I love how Saltwater Cove goes all out for Halloween. Best place to live if you ask me."

She paused stirring and glanced my way.

"I'm so glad you're back this year. *The Melting Pot* hasn't been the same without you. *I* haven't been the same without you."

The pang of sadness in her voice gripped my heart tight.

The Melting Pot is Aunt Edie's witch themed café. Her pride and joy. We'd spend hours cooking up new delicious recipes to sell to her customers. Her cooking is to die for, I guess that's where I get my passion from. My dream was always to stay in Saltwater Cove and run the business together, but she insisted I travel and experience the world. Done and dusted.

I glanced around the kitchen, my gaze landing on the empty cat bed in the corner. "Where is my mischievous familiar this morning? Doesn't she usually keep you company when you're cooking?"

Miss Saffron had been my saving grace after my parents died. She'd found me when my soul had been ripped out, when I had nothing more to live for. Thanks to her friendship, I rekindled my will to live, and love.

It isn't uncommon for a witch to have a familiar. It's kind of the norm in the witch world, but none as special as Miss Saffron. My diva familiar, of the spoilt kind. Her exotic appearance with high cheekbones and shimmering black silver-tipped coat still dazzles me. They say the Chausie breed is a distant cousin of the miniature cougar. She certainly has some fight nestled in her bones. But Miss Saffron's best features are her glamourous eyes. More oval than almond-shaped with a golden glow to rival a morning sunrise.

"Oh, I'm sure she's around somewhere. She's probably found some unexplored territory to investigate. I'm sure she'll turn up when it's time to eat or you get into mischief."

Although not completely wrong, I ignored the mischief comment. "Speaking of eating, what is that?" I asked, leaning in closer, my mouth drooling at the sweet caramel aroma. A cheeky grin spread across Aunt Edie's face.

Oh no, do I want to know?

"Well, Halloween's not for everyone and some of the kids were complaining last year certain townspeople were grumpy when they went trick or treating so it got me thinking. I thought I'd spice things up a bit this year with a happy spell."

My eyebrows went up. "A happy spell?"

She nodded and scooped a little spoonful into a pumpkin shaped candy mould. "When I'm done, we'll have cheerful candy to hand out for all the grouchy Halloween spoilers out there. Within ten seconds of popping one of these little darlings in their mouth, their frown will turn upside down and they'll be spreading the happy vibes to all. I'm going to make sure this year is as wonderful as it can be."

"Aunt Edie, you can't." My stomach dropped and I gripped the edge of the kitchen bench with one hand. The disastrous implications of her words sent shivers running down my spine. "You know it's against the law to use magic to change the essence of a person. You could be sanctioned or worse, have your powers stripped."

"Relax, sweetie," she said, pausing, her smile serene and calm. "This falls under the Halloween Amendment of 1632."

"What are you talking about...The Halloween Amendment of 1632? I've never heard of it."

A subtle puff of air escaped her lips. "Halloween wasn't exactly your favourite holiday growing up, especially after your parents died, and then you missed the last two or so travelling."

"But I was back by last Christmas."

She smiled. "Yes indeed. And it was the best Christmas ever. But Halloween was always a reminder you were different."

"Yeah, a witch."

"Yes."

She placed her hand on mine. A sigh left my lips at the warmth of her reassuring touch.

"A day when young girls dressed up as witches. Where their fantasy was your daily reality."

Aunt Edie's words were like a slap in the face with a wet dishcloth. "Was I really that self-absorbed? I'm so sorry to have dumped it all on you. I guess I was pretty hard to live with at times."

"Hard? Never," she said, her jaw gaping in mock horror. "Challenging, now that's a definite possibility."

She burst into laughter and my heart overflowed with warmth as the sweet sound filled the room.

I threw my arms around her and squeezed. "I love you, Aunt Edie."

"I love you too, sweetheart."

I pulled back and drilled my eyes into hers, wanting answers. "Now, what is this Halloween Amendment of 1632?"

Her eyes sparkled like gemstones and she resumed filling candy moulds with green slimy goo. "The amendment is only active for five days leading up to Halloween and finishes at the stroke of midnight October thirty-first. It allows any graduate or fully qualified witch to enhance the holiday using magic as long as it is temporary, no harm or foul comes to the object of the spell or intentionally alters the future."

"Are you serious? That means me. I'm a graduate witch," I said. My inner child was doing jumping jacks.

Aunt Edie tutted. "True. A graduate witch who is still learning the ropes and until you receive your full qualification at twenty-five, even then, you must always strive to be the best witch you can be. We can't afford another mishap like graduation."

If it wasn't for my three besties, Harriet, Jordi, Tyler and, Aunt Edie's guidance and training, I may never have made it to graduation. My mind skipped back to the disastrous end to the graduation party. It wasn't exactly my fault the party ended in rack and ruin. Who knew having a shapeshifter for a best friend could cause so much havoc?

I caught the upturned lip of Aunt Edie and chuckled. "Oh, come on, even you thought it was funny when Jordi shifted into a raven and chased that cow, Prudence McAvoy around the ballroom. She's had it in for Jordi ever since I moved to Saltwater Cove. I guess she pushed one too many times, I mean, no-one taunts Jordi and gets away with it." I giggled, the blood-red face of Prudence covered in banoffee pie was the best graduation present, ever. "Besides, my involvement came down to wrong place, wrong time. Prudence eventually owned up, it was all on her. But I get the message. Be a good witch."

"That's my girl." Aunt Edie huffed, dropping the spoon back in the empty pan. She wiped her sweaty brow with the back of her hand and smeared the remains of the gooey green substance on her hands down her apron. "There all done. Time to let them set."

"How do you know the spell works? I mean, will they work on everyone?" I asked.

Aunt Edie crossed her arms and pinched her lips together, her cheeks glowing a cute rosy pink. "Of course, they'll work on everyone, even those beings of the paranormal kind. Since when *hasn't* one of my spells worked, young lady?"

True. You don't earn the title of master witch by doing terrible spells that fail.

She rubbed her chin and continued. "But I wouldn't say no to testing them before Halloween rolls around."

"Have you got a guinea pig in mind?" I paused at her sly grin. "All I can say is, it better not be me."

***

Daily life was made a whole lot easier since The Melting Pot joined Aunt Edie's house. Walking next door to work suited me just fine. Kind of like an extension of her kitchen. She loved to share her passion for cooking delicious food with the rest of the world. A passion we both shared.

I twisted my wavy blue-streaked chestnut hair into a messy bun on top of my head and shoved it under my witch's hat. Glancing at my reflection, I saw it screamed modern classy-chic witch in an understated way. My dainty black satin skirt fell just above my knees showing off my trendy black and orange horizontal strip stockings. A slick black short sleeve button-up blouse fit perfectly covered in an orange vest, the words The Melting Pot embroidered above the right breast pocket in white. To add the finishing touch, I slipped my size seven feet into a pair of black lace up Doc Martin ankle boots and tied the black and silver glitter laces in elegant bows. I surveyed my reflection one last time in the mirror and grinned. I mean, who else gets to dress up every day as a witch to go to work. "Me, that's who."

An electric buzz filled my blood as I pushed open the door and stepped into The Melting Pot, closing it swiftly behind me. A clever tactic on Aunt Edie's part to design her café like a witch's cave. Everywhere I looked shouted witch heaven. Cauldrons of various sizes and candelabras standing high on their perches framed the seating area. Pumpkins scattered among the witches' brooms and replica spell books. Potions and brews strategically placed high on display shelves gave off the perfect image of a witch's cave. Best not tell anyone they're real. Aunt Edie insisted on an element of authenticity. Every child's Halloween dream all year round. I squeezed my hands together in front of my heart. "Gosh, I love my job."

A purr echoed from the floor to my right and glancing down, I saw my four-legged feline slinking elegantly in a figure eight between my legs. "You love it here too, don't you, Miss Saffron?" She stretched and catapulted up onto the counter, her agility and poise qualities to admire. Her big yellow eyes stared at me and she purred. "I swear you know exactly what I'm saying."

Aunt Edie's merry voice trailed into the main serving area from the kitchen. "I've got a wooden spoon here dripping with the last of my famous chocolate-strawberry sauce. Unless someone comes to claim it in the next ten seconds, I'll have to wash it down the sink."

"Shotgun," I whispered in Miss Saffron's direction then took off dodging tables and chairs in record time to make it to the kitchen. "Don't you dare. You know it's my favourite."

Miss Saffron sat tall on the counter, her beady eyes keeping a firm gaze on the chocolate covered spoon in my hand. My insides salivated as I licked it clean. "Oh my God. A-MA-ZING." The best part of my childhood was beating mum to the spoon and bowl when Aunt Edie was cooking up a storm. My gut clenched. I missed my mum and dad so much some days the hurt was unbearable.

The cowbell above the main entry door jingled and I jumped, startled by the unexpected intrusion. I glanced at the antique wall clock. Eight fifteen. We weren't even open yet.

"Anybody here?" Barked a familiar grouchy pompous voice.

Great. Why does today have to start with a visit from the Queen of Complaints?

"Evelyn Grayson. Stop scowling right this instant," said Aunt Edie. "You look like you're sucking a lemon. It may be fifteen minutes before we open, but you know my policy, every customer deserves a warm witch welcome."

My chest hollowed out as Aunt Edie's words curbed my inner snob. "Of course, you're right. I'm sorry," I said, dropping the spoon in the sink and wiping the chocolate sauce from my face.

"But..." Aunt Edie paused and handed me a plate. The cheeky twinkle in her eyes confused me. "It wouldn't hurt Saltwater Cove's town grouch to be happy once in a while."

I looked down at the plate and a gasped in jubilation.

Green happy candy.

"Why Aunt Edie, you are positively sinful. I love it. But I'm not even sure a happy spell will work on Camille."

"Worth a try. After all what better guinea pig could we ask for?"

I nodded and grabbed the plate. Plastering on a smile I headed out ready to see if one happy candy can soften the most bad-tempered creature I've ever had the pleasure of meeting.

"It's about time. What does a woman have to do to get service around here?" Camille Stenson snapped. "What sort of business are you running, making customers wait so long?"

I bit my tongue and held back the cynical comment chomping at the bit to get out. "I'm terribly sorry to have kept you waiting, Miss Stenson. What can I do for you?"

Her jaw dropped and a fiery shade of red washed over her pale complexion. I pursed my lips tight together to stop the laugh growing in my belly from escaping.

"It's Wednesday or have you forgotten?" She asked, her eyebrows raised, showing the stark whites of her eyes.

A shudder bolted through my body.

Scary. Yes, I know, Mr Bain's dinner, of course.

Why he can't come in and get it himself is beyond me. She's supposed to be the loan's officer at the bank, not his wife. The sarcastic tone fuelled my inner desire to squash her like a petulant fly.

Perfect guinea pig.

I eased the plate of yummy caramel scented candy in front of Camille's nose. "My sincere apologies.

Please accept one of Aunt Edie's treats as a peace offering. She made them especially for the Halloween season."

"Pfft, Halloween is a waste of time if you ask me." Camille leaned in to examine the plate and frowned. Her brows crinkled together in an unattractive monobrow. "Mmm, you're not trying to poison me, are you?"

Poison? No. Cheer you up so you can stop making everyone else miserable? Yes.

"How could you say such a thing?" I said, feigning hurt. "You know Aunt Edie's food is the best for miles around. That's why people keep coming back."

"Fine." She rolled her hazel eyes to the roof, huffed, and popped a candy in her mouth.

I stood frozen, waiting, my pulse pulverising my temples as if I was standing on the edge of a cliff ready to jump. One…two…three…four. Camille stared at me, her hazel eyes clouding over. Five…six…seven. Nothing, absolutely nothing. Eight…nine. My eye caught Aunt Edie peeking in from the kitchen and she shrugged. I guess it doesn't work on people whose core being is made up of such deep-set crankiness. Ten.

"Evelyn, my dear precious Evelyn." Camille's tone shot three octaves higher. A smile flashed across her face as electric as a neon sign in the dead of night.

"You look positively radiant as always. I never seem to tell you enough how beautiful you are. Just like your mother. God rest her soul."

My mother? How did she know my mother?

I swear I'd been transported into an alternate universe. "Um, thank you. That is kind of you to say. But how…"

"Pfft, nonsense," she interrupted with a sashaying movement of her hand. "It so great to have you back in Saltwater Cove. I bet your aunt is pleased you're home?"

Did she mention my mother? Maybe I imagined it. I made a mental note to follow up Camille's comment about my mother with Aunt Edie.

"I…." Stunned by Camille's reaction to the spell, my words caught in the back of my throat.

"That I am," Aunt Edie said, threading an arm around my waist. With her head turned from Camille's view, she gave me a cheeky wink.

She handed a paper bag to Camille and smiled. "Here you go, Mr Bain's dinner. His usual, just how he likes it."

"Perfect. He doesn't know how good he has it eating your wonderful meals four nights a week. He's off to some big Banking Symposium at Dawnbury Heights this afternoon but insisted I still pick up his dinner so he can take it with him. He can't stand hotel food, mind you, who can? Makes him all bloated." Camille said, placing the food inside a bigger tapestry carpet bag.

It kind of reminded me of Mary Poppins' bottomless bag. She turned toward the exit and waved.

"Ta-ta now. You ladies have a wonderful day, and may it be filled with all the magical wonders of the world."

The cow bell rattled as she left. My jaw dropped, and I stared at the closed door in silence. I looked at Aunt Edie and within seconds we were both into hysterical fits of laughter.

"Well I'd say...that spell...is a winner, wouldn't you?" I said, barely able to speak between giggles.

She nodded and cleared her throat wiping a tear from her eye. "I hope she stays that way for the next hour and a half. But who knows, it all depends on the individual person."

I laughed so much a stitch stabbed my side. "Aw," I said, pressing against the pain. "Okay, I give up, why do we want it to last an hour and a half?"

"Because Vivienne has an appointment with Camille in about thirty minutes regarding her loan application. If all goes well, she'll be able to expand her business just like she's always planned."

Vivienne Delany and Aunt Edie have been best friends since primary school. Aunt Edie ran The Melting Pot and Vivienne was the proud owner of *Perfect Pumpkin Home-Made Treats* where she made every kind of dish out of pumpkins one could dare to conjure up. And even though they both ran food business; they'd die before letting harm come to the other. That's what best friends do for each other.

"Let hope your spell does the trick." The cow bell jiggled over the door, signalling the beginning of the morning rush. "I guess we'll have to wait and see."

Lightning Source UK Ltd.
Milton Keynes UK
UKHW010644170822
407432UK00002B/365